C
Knows the Words

Roz Paterson

Polygon

© Roz Paterson, 2002

Polygon
An imprint of Edinburgh University Press Lttd
22 George Square, Edinburgh

Typeset in Galliard by Hewer Text Ltd, Edinburgh, and
printed and bound in Great Britain by
Creative Print & Design, Ebbw Vale, Wales

A CIP record for this book is
available from the British Library

ISBN 0 7486 6320 7 (paperback)

To Malcolm

L ast year, my friend left her husband. She didn't love him and realised she might have time to find someone she did. So far, she's been disappointed.

She's a good-looking woman in her early forties, but the men she bumps into in bars or gets offered by dating agencies seem to be either pensionable or certifiable. It's no mystery why they're single, let's put it that way.

Being a bit of a body-fascist, she hardly relishes the prospect of her Clarins-cosseted body being embraced by one in the grip of liver spots, or her lively spirit being dampened down by golf handicaps and corn plasters.

These old boys smoke Craven A and carry engraved gold lighters. One used to call her simply 'Girl' and he didn't even mean to be offensive. Such encounters lead her to believe she prefers the company of library books.

Others are less tweed waistcoat, more straitjacket.

She dated, even though dating sounds too cheerleaderish a word for this exercise in mental intimidation, a fifty-eight-year-old musician with a clipped grey beard. He took her to dimly lit restaurants where he chain-smoked and studied her while she ate, occasionally interjecting some cod-Freudian analysis of her conversation and bearing.

After five such encounters I took her to Durham and told her to get a grip. Three nights, one of which she spent with a student engineer, later and she did.

As often happens with misguided affairs of the heart, the musician took the loss badly and conducted a bitter telephone campaign until LoveLines Inc fed him another lonely wench with too many cat-themed cushions.

At first, I was fascinated by the human flotsam she encountered but soon developed a preference for the edited highlights only.

Until, that is, she told me she was going out with Charlie McGuigan. She wasn't to know the resonance this name had for me, that it set off a reaction like servants' bells ringing of their own volition up and down the corridors of an abandoned country manor.

And she didn't seem to notice the hysterical note in the questions I fired at her.

Thank Christ, he was the wrong age, wrong profession, wrong height, looks and marital status but I couldn't, God help me, be sure.

I wondered if it was the approach of the menopause that was doing this to me as I pulled up in front of the smoked glass windows of her favourite Italian bistro, waiting for my friend to arrive in her mini-cab.

This wasn't his kind of place, this riot of chalkboards and neon lights, and what would I do if it was him anyway? I was wearing the kind of clothes I'd always sworn I'd never wear – dungarees and a quilted anorak for starters – and I was married with children and a well-tended garden to think of.

I scoured the men on the step. One was four and looked queasy – the other was stout and middle-aged and carried a fussy little telescopic umbrella in his hands even though it hadn't rained in two months.

When she drove up, the umbrella man seemed to move forward but then another man appeared. Taller, less Hercule Poirot in aspect but not, not my Charlie.

I laid my head on my hands over the steering wheel and closed my eyes. I felt the old impulse to drive the car, anywhere and everywhere, until I found him. Until, exhausted, grey and withered, I found him.

Instead I drove home, loaded the washing machine, made myself a pot of coffee and stayed up half the night editing a scene between two travelling salesmen who meet by chance in a station buffet during the 1960s.

This is what he wanted for me so this is what he gets.

I haven't seen Charlie for twenty years and I don't expect I ever will again. Bella's mention of the name was as startling as an emergency stop in a car. But there was no damage done.

Ironically, the whole thing with me and him was born of desperation. I turned to Charlie because I had no one else. But for all its unlikeliness, it proved to be the hinge that connects the two halves of my life. From where I floundered, he hauled me up to the light.

BC – Before Charlie – and AD – After David.

There are still some people who insist it was a silly misadventure between a dirty old man and a jilted teenager but, all grown up and away now, I think I'm the better judge.

1

We met on a beautiful, late summer night. That fact lends it overtones of destiny but the detail is altogether more clumsy. Sunlight the colour of dark orange squash rendered the landscape in rich, oil paint colours. Parched grass turned into lush, sad green while the dried mud tracks that scarred the fields blushed in terracotta.

Midgies gathered in puffballs under trees and wherever the underground streams broke surface, ambushing you as you walked past. While the sheep meandered mournfully, I tamped down a piece of turf by the roadside and watched my boyfriend, together with all my friends, leave me behind.

I was eighteen, five foot ten and what my minuscule mother called 'of solid build'. I should have been en route to a seaside barbecue, to eat charred sausages, drink warm cans of beer and play rounders in the dark. As it happened, I was relegated to the sidelines while my social and love life revved its engines in readiness to depart.

A broad sunburnt face full of freckles grinned and said, with faltering bonhomie, that I'd be missing myself as he rubbed sweat from his forehead with his upper arm and examined the middle distance.

My boyfriend David shrugged approximately in my direction, uncomfortably aware that my reason for staying was sitting beside him. She was called Lorraine and, to my mind, exuded a kind of bovine stubbornness by way of a personality. I hated her for having the temerity not only to have sex with someone else's – that is my – official boyfriend, but not even to feel bad about it. Needless to say, I hated my friends for tolerating her existence, never mind her participation in this annual social event.

Julia Donald, my best friend, swivelled her hips to a song on the radio, winked at me, and got into a van with the freckled creature. She was wearing her hey-don't-be-so-serious look like a bad wig.

The convoy rolled into life and a still bright ball of sunlight bounced across the windscreens as they turned, one by one, onto the main road.

Someone blithely tooted their horn in farewell and my hand rose to wave of its own accord.

I waited for someone to execute a screeching U-turn and insist I came along, or insist on staying with me, but no such someone bothered. I was left behind like a Christmas puppy in a layby, my heart flapping inside my chest and my eyes blinking furiously.

Eventually I turned for home.

In the murky light I spied my mother, gazing sleepily into one of her trashy weekly mags.

She lifted her eyes in my direction as I walked in but, seconds later, had resumed her lethargic reading.

'This woman poured boiling water over her toyboy's privates,' she said tonelessly. I knew precisely how this woman felt as I rooted through the kitchen cupboards for something to cram into my mouth.

'There's cheese,' my mother said.

There was just the two of us in the hut. It had been built in a spirit of optimism as a holiday chalet sometime back in the 1950s. Doubtless the architect had fondly imagined its floors resounding to the footfalls of blonde children who liked jigsaws and kites, not a shabby mother-and-daughter twosome who came here because it was cheap.

We lived in a park full of other such chalets. In summer, as now, it throbbed to the beat of ghetto blasters and crying toddlers, while in winter the doors and windows shut up like slapped faces and grim silence took hold.

It made no difference to us. We bickered when we had the energy and the rest of the time we got by with a kind of companionable enmity.

Don't get me wrong. I loved my mother very deeply. When I thought about her life and her ferocious, misplaced loyalties, I felt something bordering on passion. It was just the irritating, petty-minded reality of her that I couldn't stand.

So I stood leaning over the sink eating a cheese sandwich, with the cheese twice as thick as the bread, glowering at a tubby little girl pegging tea-towels to a guy rope. Mum stirred and said that she was going out to see poor old Deborah in the village.

You could easily get the impression that she and Deborah were soul sisters, the amount of time they spent together. But of course, they did no such thing.

Deborah was deaf and only opened the door when the delivery boy from William Low called by with her weekly supply of Jamaica Ginger Cake and Spam. Actually, I wasn't too sure if she was even still alive.

Deceased or otherwise, she was the ideal alibi for those seeking illicit rendezvous with married men. In my mother's case, with a certain Frankie McAllister, whose wife lived in the family home on the mainland while he stayed in his island hotel.

I don't know how the marriage worked. It was perfectly possible that they hated each other enough to find this arrangement pleasant.

I nodded at Mum, while gulping scalding coffee to which I'd added far too much sugar. I don't know what my hurry was, but I remember eating and drinking like I was winning a pie-eating contest.

All too soon my sandwich had been transferred from my hand to some ledge just above my breastbone. And, much as I'd have liked to spend the evening beating my chest in the interests of comfortable digestion, Mum wouldn't leave till I did – for fear I'd notice she wasn't walking in the direction of Deborah's house – so I had to go out.

I walked in the direction of the Drumclair Inn, possibly with the notion that David might be there waiting for me. That he might have shaken off twenty-six years of conditioning and rural Scottish prejudice and realised that he wanted a fine mind for his companion, not a fat girl who took a generous cup size and agreed with him all the time.

David. I was sixteen to his twenty-four when we became a couple. Like all things round here, I'd known it was going to happen weeks before it actually did.

Julia sprawled across the floor of her bedroom, a grotto of unaired linen and tatty David Essex pics, and tittered over her *My Guy*.

'David Gunn's after you,' she said, before skiting off onto the more interesting topic of who was after her.

I pleaded with her to tell me more but she simply raised her eyebrows and said all she knew was that we should be at the Royal Stuart that evening. I'd never really noticed David before but, like many teenage girls, I could fancy at will.

He never showed up that night and failed to actually make his clumsy first move for weeks on end. By which time I was so coiled up with excitement and impatience I thought he was Clark Gable.

He was the usual permanently embarrassed, bluff country boy in many ways. He never said anything nice to me and only held my hand when he was extremely drunk and needed the support.

But he paid for everything, even when I had money. In exchange I had to put up with us being surrounded by local girls of his own age who bristled over the fact that their 'Davie' was going out with a city girl.

I was from Dundee originally, ladies and gentlemen. No crack cocaine dealing city slicker was I – but I suppose, if you've spent your life wearing clothes from the Marshall Ward catalogue and getting your blonde streaks done by your frustrated, grossly overweight second cousin, someone like me probably seemed pretty exotic. After all, I often knew what day of the week it was.

*   *   *

So there we'd be – me, him and at least half a dozen girls flirting in a possessive, big sister kind of way whilst taking turns to sit on his knee.

I usually wound up on the sidelines, drinking steadily and talking to the barstaff until I became angry enough to lurch out into the night. And he would follow, some distance behind, whining, 'Karen, oh for fuck's sake, Karen . . .'

By the time we got home he usually had me convinced I was a hormonally poisoned harridan and he and his coven of admirers reasonable people. No wonder I woke to Sundays with a hangover you could smell in Wales.

Our relationship wasn't all big nights out of course. Occasionally, well twice, he took me for a meal and I got upset and cried both times. Mainly because he suggested we break up when I tried to talk about 'us'.

'We' weren't a big success but I still thought I'd marry him, I really did. Back in BC, my expectations were so low they scraped along the sea bed.

David liked me because I came with no strings attached. Other boyfriends had to put up with girlfriends' families. One bit of bad behaviour and a barrage of angry aunties and censorious cousins would chivvy them into line, make them get engaged and stop them going to the pub.

All I had was Mum and she would hide when someone knocked on the door so David could, and did, behave as he liked.

Like I said, I wasn't local. We'd moved here after my dad left for a new life as an unemployed person in Blackheath. These days he was dividing his time between cab-driving and decorating rundown tenancies in South Norwood.

I was briefly heart-broken at losing my daddy but, being a resilient girl, the idea of living in a holiday home all year round quite revived me.

I made friends with a girl called Corina – known as Corrie – who was built like a fawn and had a dappled complexion to

8

match. Despite her delicate body she was rough and foul-mouthed (she was the first girl I knew to say 'arsehole') and very, very good at schoolwork.

She was hit by a car when she was twelve and never regained consciousness. She'd been walking home from a party, all dolled up in green tights and red buckle shoes, her hair fused into two little Heidi plaits. The car hit her at 70 mph and I wasn't allowed to see the body.

There was a funeral service at which I sat frozen beside my classmates. We sang 'Onward Christian Soldiers', her favourite hymn (actually no, her favourite was 'We Three Kings' but the timing was against her – it was January), and a girl called Samantha, whose sole contact with Corrie had been kicking her under the schooldesk, cried so vehemently that she was taken outside and given a Curly-Wurly. I looked up at a stained-glass St Peter and silently asked him why Corrie had left me to this.

Shortly after the funeral, her mum and dad moved away. Shortly after that, they broke up and her mum married someone else and moved to Ireland. I could understand that, even then. What could be worse than having a dead daughter between you?

And Corrie stayed behind, going green in the darkness of her coffin.

2

M aking the best of a bad lot, I immediately befriended Julia
Donald. Unfortunately her closest associate was Suzanna
Williams, who didn't like my being around at all. But I managed
because, like all lonely children, I just hung in there and let them
hide my mittens or tell everyone I'd deposited solids in my
knickers whenever their faltering friendship required it.

By the time we reached our mid-teens it had almost become a
three-way thing. As one we'd study *Cosmopolitan* quizzes like
they were chemistry textbooks and tear out the seams of our jeans
and restitch them so tightly they wound round our legs like the
chute on a helter skelter. We fought all the time too, one or other
of us flaring down the stairs with a red face and a string of
expletives trailing from our lips like air bubbles streaming from
the mouth of a fish. And then we'd make up, via a series of
diplomatic phone calls and a few hesitant smiles across the desks
at school. But the old first friend loyalty remained, even though
Julia and I were so much more alike than Julia and Suzanna. Even
though Suzanna said, at the age of fourteen, that she wanted to
get married and have six children and live in a smart new council
house like her cousin Debbie, and never changed her mind. Even
though, when I said I'd shag Mr MacInnes but only if I didn't
have to look at his face (we were playing one of those 'how far
would you go?' games and I think there was a million pounds at
stake), Julia shrieked with laughter and Suzanna looked at me
quizzically and later warned Julia not to slag Mr MacInnes

because it was obvious I had feelings for him. That loyalty, forged across their mothers' doorsteps and the yellow plastic seats of swings, remained as potent as a first language and nothing about me could supersede those first words and deep-rooted vowel sounds. Which is why, when I was abandoned at the roadside by David, Julia stuck with the herd.

So back to this night, in the late summer of my eighteenth year, when I met Charlie. I had found out about Lorraine by ear-wigging into a conversation in the toilets at work. Back then I worked in a café, an establishment famed for its drop scones and overriding smell of butter and boiled ham.

It was part of a brave little seafront terrace overlooking the ferry pier and, on a clear day, had a passable view of the mainland. As well as our blue painted facade, there was the Spar, Frankie McAllister's Royal Stuart Hotel, a post office bulging with footballs and plastic jewellery sets and a rotten little chemist's with yellow cellophane lining the inside of the windows. It sold pain-killers and prescription drugs and nothing else. Not even those little rectangular lollies that are supposedly good for you. God, I hated that shop.

Everyone on the island passed by this terrace every day of their lives and seemed to dispense all their secrets, not over a warming cup of tea, but over the raucous belch of the café toilets' hand-dryers.

If you wanted to know who was ruining their life and reputation by bedding whom, then all you had to do was park yourself in one of those cubicles and wait.

I had heard all kinds of tat within those walls – much of which I solemnly repeated to whoever cared to listen – but this was the first time I'd ever heard anything featuring me. Except that it didn't feature me. At all.

Perhaps that was the worst of it. The two voices, one of which belonged to Suzanna, discussed the fact that David and Lorraine had been collapsing drunkenly onto fold-out beds for more than three weeks now, without once mentioning the fact that I might in any way be upset or, indeed, that I even existed.

11

'She's a dog,' Suzanna commented in her apple-sweet voice.

'Aye, a bike,' her companion Anne-Marie agreed in an altogether harder, less wholesome manner.

And me? What about me?

'But she's worth keeping in with – her gran's crackin' at making up dress patterns,' added the ever practical Anne-Marie.

'Too right,' said Suzanna falteringly, sounding like a fawn that's been bullied into shooting a baby rabbit.

And that was that. My part in the affair was, it appeared, negligible. Oddly, the bad news sustained me through what could have been an interminable afternoon. For some reason, bad news stimulated me in a way that good news never could. Accidents, disasters and betrayals gave my heart a little kick-start while good stuff just seemed to cement the status quo, making me feel that my tiny world was truly without end.

The last dregs of the tourist season slurped up the last dregs of their tea while a wasp drizzled amongst the dried flower displays in the window. I wandered around spilling cold beverages from abandoned cups and, every once in a while, bravely contemplated my misfortune, like it was a spectacular injury sustained heroically in front of the whole school.

In a way, I was quite thrilled – it was one of the biggest things that had ever happened to me.

However, as I took off my apron at six o'clock I realised that by now everyone would know. I could run wailing down the pier if I fancied but it was yesterday's chip paper to everyone else. Get a life, they'd say – oblivious to the fact that they were slowly boring themselves to death.

I went to Julia's straight from work.

When I told her about David she said, without a hint of surprise, that yes, he was a right one, wasn't he, as she packed her eyelash curlers into the sidepocket of her Wild Rover rucksack. Her mouth formed a tender, but impersonally so, oval when I said I wasn't going.

Suzanna arrived at my heels and suggested I buy myself a bottle of Southern Comfort and jump the bones of the first man I met.

I considered smacking her hard across the face but plumped for a more mature response and told her she was a silly bitch (and I'd always hated her).

And then, a few hours later, I found myself at the door of the Drumclair, the bar that served the High Street – and anyone from the age of ten upwards. It was currently devoid of anyone under forty. The barmaid said was I not going, and wasn't that crazy, she would if she was my age. I ordered a Southern Comfort, which hissed though my boiling gut and made me feel instantly sick, and stared blindly at 'Fiona sux cocks' carved onto the chair in front of me.

There was a group of men stationed in the window with dominoes protruding from their clenched fists like cartoon claws from the paws of a cat. A voice from their midst cautioned me to steady on – I'd only had one! – or I'd put Charlie to shame.

And then he was there. Dressed in a pair of ancient denims and a Guinness T-shirt, with a pair of scraggy sideburns meandering down his cheeks. Charlie McGuigan. He was David's step-uncle, that is, the brother of David's stepdad. I didn't know much about him, other than that he looked like a roadie.

But he won my heart the moment he spoke because what he said was, 'They're a bunch of cruel wee bastards.'

3

He may have been a bit rough around the edges, but Charlie was bordering on the dream date. Not that he was a date. Oh no, and I put enormous effort into my body language to make that clear. I didn't want this old man getting ideas.

But he was one of the first men I'd met who could say more than 'aye, aye' whenever he caught my eye – the usual girl/boy fare in my experience. We girls would absorb American high school films featuring teenagers, both male and female, pouring their hearts out to each other, only to be disappointed when our boys failed to get beyond eulogising on the merits of 'Bat Out Of Hell'.

Cross-gender communication was not something we did in this part of the world.

Except for Charlie. He did communication in a big way.

We sat together at the bar and the previously snotty barmaid suddenly turned into Mrs Friendly. She even gave us free drinks.

I hadn't intended to but he was such an encouraging listener that I told him all about it. Not in an ordered narrative but in fits and starts. 'It's just that he's such a wanker . . .' or 'What really bugs me is that . . .' while poor old Charlie manfully put a caring face on it.

'I wasn't any better at that age,' he admitted.

'So it's alright then?' I demanded in reply, my vodka and orange slopping over the rim of its glass.

I don't know why he bothered really, it couldn't have been much fun for him.

'Of course, he's a wanker . . .' I started up again like a weary engine but was stopped by Charlie's laying his hand on my forearm and taking my glass from my hand. It had shattered, probably against the bar, without my even noticing.

He opened up my hand to check for glass splinters and I was momentarily quietened by his unexpected gentleness.

Later, as it neared the official closing time, he sat back and asked me, looking deep into my eyes – or he could just have been trying to focus – to tell him about myself.

I couldn't resist, despite my reservations about this man's unsuitability. So I told him all about myself, freely ad-libbing in a bid not to sound as dull as I really was.

I don't think it would have mattered. I think my voice served as a kind of musical accompaniment to drinking and I can't remember what I said and I'm sure he had no idea either.

We went on to a party. One of those parties that Charlie and his friends seemed to have at the rustle of an off-licence carrier-bag. Certainly no one looked even mildly surprised when we turned up at a house at the end of the village in the small hours of the morning with a bottle of Bells and six cans of Tartan Special.

The woman who answered the door, Lizzie Long, looked to be about a hundred and forty. She barked at me and cuffed Charlie round the ear by way of a hello and led us into a dim living-room upholstered in various stages of broken down humanity. Forty-something men and a light smattering of similarly aged women sat and stood, smoking and drinking like their lives depended on it.

Some looked up in baffled enquiry and some made a murmuring attempt at our names.

A Pink Floyd tape played very quietly in a corner while a tall man sang 'Danny Boy' before tottering backwards into a chair.

I made my way to a squashy beige leather sofa where the sitters parted like the Red Sea. Charlie followed and practically sat on top of a hefty sleeping man to his right.

A man with an odd beard began to sing 'My Way' very slowly and mournfully. I say began, because his progress was hampered by his inability to remember what came after 'too few to mention'.

15

'Oh Jesus Christ Almighty,' sighed Charlie. But his critique was cut short by Lizzie Long commanding him to sing.

'Charlie'll show you how it's done,' she rasped, 'He knows the words.'

It was seven o'clock in the morning when we left. We walked unsteadily through the too bright morning listening to the birds singing. The ground was damp with dew and I wondered if my mother would be up yet. Or if she was even home.

At my door Charlie ruffled my hair and smiled a tired, slightly sozzled smile.

'Don't stay up too late,' he said, before shambling back to the road. Just before he disappeared from view he turned and saluted like a captain going down with his ship. I saluted back.

I woke up at two o'clock the following afternoon and it hit me like a bag of sand. Charlie McGuigan! I'd spent the evening with Charlie McGuigan and he probably thought we were going out with each other now. And he'd probably already told everybody we'd had sex.

I spent the day in the house, waiting for my toes to uncurl.

The male youths and their wretched female accomplices came back on the Sunday. Julia called round at the house but I didn't answer because I knew she wanted to rib me about Charlie.

They'd all know. That woman at the Drumclair would have been cackling about it over the gin and oranges all morning, the old witch. And the girls would be telling David they'd been right about me all along and he'd be shuddering at just how low down on the evolutionary scale his replacement was.

I was very vain when I was eighteen, in that hysterical, oh-my-god-they're-looking kind of way. I couldn't bear to look silly or be laughed at. But for all that, I wasn't unkind. If Charlie had called round that night I wouldn't have been ghastly to him – I'd just have told him that it was 'too soon' and I 'wasn't ready to commit to anyone'. I really had seen a lot of American high school films.

Needless to say, he didn't. The only person who ventured my way was my mother and she was so grumpy and hungover I felt like throwing her into the main road.

16

4

I didn't leave the chalet park till Wednesday. I tended to stay holed up for long periods of time as a matter of course even though it made me feel helpless and depressed and it took a huge effort to come to life again.

I'd come out of hiding and find myself being startled by the ferocity of the sea air as I turned the corner of the road and took in the pier and the few remaining boats rocking in the harbour like flotsam.

It was a cold day, signalling the end of the season, and the sky was mottled with white clouds. Nothing was happening and nothing would, for ages.

At the café my absence was unremarked on. I sometimes wondered if they actually knew I worked there or just thought I came in a lot.

Leandra, nominally my boss, sang out one of the 'good mornings' she dispensed to the public, noticed it was me, said 'oh', laughed, and sang out 'good morning' in exactly the same voice.

She was intent on one of her vastly complex yet unsatisfying dried flower arrangements. Despite the colours she used and the ribbons she wound, they all came out brown and dusty and terribly dead. They filled the windows, covered the walls and choked the bric-à-brac like a malevolent, prehistoric algae.

Her mania was borne of her need to be good at something. When anyone remarked that she had a talent, that her efforts were in any way worthwhile, she purred like a stroked cat. The rest of the time she was little and clumsy and generally bad at things.

Meantime Mary, her elderly mother, ploughed on with her mammoth roll-buttering duties, pausing briefly to wield her trusty bone-handled knife in a military-style salute.

The café smelled nice in the morning. Mary always kept the doors wide open to disperse the stale odour of ham that seemed to haunt the place while Jimmy, the delivery man, stopped by to make us all coffee.

It was really rather nice coffee he made, in his touchingly fussy way, with his own cafetière that he kept under our sink.

Jimmy was over seventy and his entire career revolved around the delivering of rolls and milk to various establishments scattered across the island.

Despite this less than lucrative lifestyle, he afforded two months every year in Naples, where he boarded at the same guesthouse, worked his way through the region's winelists and painted blurry, atmospheric little watercolours that he only showed to people when he was drunk at New Year. He never attempted to sell them and he never painted when he was home. Instead he made coffee and smiled quietly to himself.

Perhaps he was more gregarious with the 'Napoleons' as David used, rather tiresomely, to refer to them.

Neither Lea, nor Mary nor Jimmy said a word about Charlie and I began to relax. Maybe the old fella was more discreet, and less desperate, than I gave him credit for.

Chances are he was. It was just that the people I used to refer to as friends were not. Julia was the first to appear at lunchtime, flushed from sprinting all the way from her chambermaid duties to unburden her curiosity.

'Karen!' she shrieked. 'Have you been having it away with Charlie McGuigan?'

His name rang out like that of some long forgotten vaudeville act. Charlie McGuigan. Charlie McGuigan and his amazing dancing monkey, the raggy little thing that leapt up and down in a frenzy while its lord and master ground away at the organ and grinned a freakshow grin of missing teeth and rank breath.

I cringed to my spleen and made a grotesque attempt at frivolity.

'Noooo, for God's sake.'

'Well, what in the name of God were you doing with him then? He's . . .' she paused to flick through her vast vocabulary, 'He's old!'

I realised that Anne Marie, the blunt frump I'd overheard in the toilets, and Suzanna were gathering at her shoulder which meant that I was well and truly in for a teasing. A horrible, horrible teasing.

Not that they said much. When you're mortified, people only have to wink and say his name to make you feel like you've been stabbed.

Their voices clattered round the room like rattling crockery as I fled to the kitchen to collect their ham salad baps. Of course I should just have laughed along and defused the whole thing but it wasn't even as if I was being teased about someone plausible. I mean, it was Charlie.

On the way home I looked round nervously for any figure that could possibly be him and, in so doing, ran straight into David.

He smiled at me sheepishly, said, 'Aye, aye,' and dodged past.

For hours afterwards I analysed that 'Aye, aye'. Was it an 'Aye, aye – was he good then? In the sack?' or an 'Aye, aye – I know you're devastated but that's going a bit far' or a just a straightforward, on-the-level 'Aye, aye'?

At home my mother and I sat side by side on the fold-down bed watching an entire night's-worth of TV. We barely said a word. Every time she attempted to say anything, or breathed like she was about to attempt to say anything, I let out a deep sigh and looked at the floor.

We hadn't fallen out – this was how we were.

You may wonder why I was so lazy. I suppose I daydreamed most of the time, and had myself convinced that something would happen to me to change everything.

Everyone was like that.

My job was monotonous and woefully badly paid but changing my circumstances seemed a Herculean effort that I just wasn't capable of making.

I remember waking up sometimes in the early morning with a dry, slightly choking feeling in my throat and not being able to get back to sleep. Now I recognise it as panic.

The week dragged through to Friday, when Julia insisted I came out for a drink with 'the girls'. I hated nights out with 'the girls' – mainly because I'd never felt like part of it – but I went anyway. My social diary had many vacant windows, shall we say.

I met Julia, Suzanna, Anne-Marie, who was Lea's stepdaughter and actually only about a year younger than her, Lea and her cousin Myra in the upstairs of the Royal Stuart. It was stuffy and upholstered in Hammer Horror red. It smelled of vinegar and gin and we surveyed the menus without hope.

After the usual baked potatoes all round arrived, the talk began. And it began badly, with Lea telling me all about Charlie's ex-wife. Lea wasn't quite at one with the rest of humanity. She made assumptions and ran with them where other people would have kept their mouths shut. Thus she talked up weddings where no such understanding existed; and children, as yet unconceived, were born, named and sent to one or other of the two island schools.

She told me his ex was a 'selfish woman' who had left him with loads of debts, taking it for granted that this information was important to me. 'Don't get saddled with Kate's financial affairs,' she advised and I nodded because there wasn't any point in protesting.

Julia gave Lea a 'shut up' smile and ordered a bottle of white wine. This meant she wanted us to dig in for the night. It meant she had something to say and I held my breath, hoping for a pregnancy, divorce or bigamy. I was disappointed. She simply wanted to gossip about Lorraine.

'She just thinks we're all going to be friends just because she's going out with David. I don't bloody well think so and he just ups and leaves her with us, like we're going to baby-sit.'

'Was it a bad weekend?' I asked gently, taking an ungainly mouthful of wine.

Julia snorted, 'It was the worst. I've a good mind to leave them to it next time. Bob can go if he wants but I'm not bothering.'

At this Suzanna raised her eyebrows in alarm. Of course Julia wouldn't do any such thing. Bob, after all, had a decent bit of farm coming to him. It was the only farm on the island and, in fact, the only worthwhile going concern on the island. Let him out your sight for a minute and that nice little earner could fall to the next girl he slept with without a condom.

The more I heard about Lorraine, the better I felt. Her sheer awfulness fanned my outrage, which felt a whole lot better than rejection. Julia got her teeth into the subject, possibly for the benefit of my poor, bruised little ego. Suzanna, failing to cotton on to the fact that this was female bonding at its most earnest and not a matter-of-fact recounting of a weekend outing, interjected softly that, 'You had a good chat with her though, the two of you were laughing away like hyenas.' At which Julia changed course like a speeding train, snicking smoothly across the rails without losing an iota of momentum.

'Well, what can you do? The men round here, if you didn't laugh about them, you'd kill them,' she said.

Within an hour all the island men were on the brink of being dumped and the women's movement about to experience a serious north of the border booster jag.

'I think I'd be much happier living with women. Just women. And no men,' said Julia, inspired by the spirit of Black Tower.

Of course, all this consciousness-raising ceased when Suzanna informed us, on returning from the loos, that the men were downstairs.

Needless to say, no one was dumped, apart from me, but I believed I was getting used to it.

I slept in Julia's spare bed while she and Bob clumsily attempted to have sex in the room next door. The sounds didn't make me feel lonely. In fact, they had quite the opposite effect. I'd endured enough boring, drunken humping with David and I was beginning to like having my body to myself.

21

It was a good night all in all. I slept heavily and heartily and woke up with puffy eyes and a searing headache.

And then nothing much happened for weeks. The summer was gone and the tourists returned safely to their city flats, their unpacked suitcases back up on top of their wardrobes and their cats back from the vets. And we were left to ourselves again.

My mother seemed more fretful than usual. She gave up reading her magazines and instead took to cleaning the house obsessively and ironing everything she could get her hands on.

She told me, in her distracted way, that she was going to get to grips with the place and then ended up abandoning it every weekend for the arms of Frankie McAllister.

I tried to work most weekends if I could. I had an idea about saving up money and going on holiday somewhere or even visiting Dad. He wrote once or twice and suggested I do that. It almost became an ambition of mine.

We got rain in September and after it the sky became a permanent overhang of grey cloud. I tried to imagine Blackheath as an inviting location but I could only think of rows of grey houses and skips in the streets, full of rubble.

Then Jocky had a party. Jocky was David's older brother and I really quite liked him. Not in a fancying way, you understand. But he was nice and I was invited.

A crowd of us met up in the Drumclair beforehand to ensure we didn't commit the social no-no of turning up sober. The girls sat on their boyfriends' knees, apart from Lea who sat solemnly beside her wordless giant of a husband, Mick.

David and Lorraine had the decency to stay at Jocky's and keep out of the way for now but I knew I'd have to meet them. Either that or do the unthinkable and go home to an empty chalet in the middle of an empty chalet park.

We left the pub and walked into a rain that swept the road in sheets. We broke into a canter, bottles clinking in our carrier bags, high heels clattering along the tarmac. Jocky appeared in the road in front of his house and threw me over his shoulder in a

22

fireman's lift because I was the 'only unclaimed wench', kicking the door open with his foot.

I was so out of breath and so wet that it took me a while to notice, once I was on my own two feet again, that Charlie was standing right in front of me.

He was grinning. The sight of him gave me a shock and my heart jumped. Despite myself I looked round to see if anyone was looking.

Charlie must have realised because his grin became fixed.

He handed me a bottle of Rolling Rock and asked how I was. I mumbled that I was fine and he looked as if he was going to give the conversation one more try but gave up, saying he'd see me later.

I was dismissed and I supposed it served me right. Then Jocky was at my side, trying to persuade me to join him in the shambling Gay Gordons that had broken out in the front room.

It was a great party. It got royally out of hand and whisky and red wine flowed across the carpet while Julia fell asleep in a chair and Jocky took the floor for a series of slurred songs in which every second word had been substituted with a swear.

'I'm not sure arse is a verb,' complained one of his few listeners, who attempted to stem the flow of Jocky's minstrelling by tugging his legs and making him fall over.

I wasn't doing too well myself by the time I spied David and Lorraine. I found out later that they'd been out for dinner with her parents – something he had never done with me, not that my parent was the sort of person you had dinner with. A slanging match over a half-bottle of gin was more her mode of getting to know you.

I'd been laughing, I was in mid-hysterical gurgle and Jocky was attempting to get to his feet by holding onto my waist. And there they were. Holding hands. Holding hands! And David's face loomed before mine as he said to his brother, 'Looks like you're in luck at last, my son.'

And Jocky laughed and noisily kissed one of my hands, a sensation akin to being nuzzled by some kind of wet-nosed farm

23

animal. And I fell silent, I couldn't help it, and gawped at Lorraine who had turned the colour of a tomato.

There followed a few quarters of an hour or so of me ordering Jocky to get me more drinks and I became unhappily animated, wanting David to see how happy I was while trying to ward off Jocky's advances.

I don't know how I disentangled myself but I'm sure I shoved him, and not very playfully. I've got this image of him lurching and laughing like a big drunk bear.

Eventually I found myself sitting on the doorstep with no idea of the time. It was still raining but I was flushed with drink and noise and I fancied the quiet and the cold.

I must have been drunker than I thought because I didn't notice him until he offered me a cigarette.

'Thanks Charlie,' I said.

I didn't usually smoke but it seemed like a better idea than having another sip of my tired red wine.

'How are you now?' he asked. 'You look good.'

Oddly enough I didn't squirm when he said that. His voice sounded so familiar, like something nice from years ago.

'I feel much better. I'm going on holiday. It's just, you know, my mum.' But I got no further. The cigarette caused my stomach to revolve like the drum of a washing machine and I stood up and doubled over and was sick all over the step.

Charlie had his arms round me, leading me to a bed. My head was splitting and I could feel my legs buckling.

Charlie was putting a glass of water and a bucket by the bed. I blinked and the room went dark.

Charlie was gone. I was in bed. It was dawn and I could hear seagulls.

5

I n mid-November the weather closed in, so that we became like a raft adrift on the North Sea. It was always like this, the skies bulked over with cloud and the air turned still and wretchedly cold. Because there was barely an hour of visibility across the water, the mainland – and with it, the rest of the world – ceased to exist.

Every winter I resigned myself to the feeling that I was here forever. But I tried very hard to make this an exception. I really did.

For one, I went on a diet. Not a very serious one, more what the magazines call a healthy eating plan. I laboured my way through bags of tasteless apples and ate baked potatoes without butter every night. It would have driven my mother to distraction if she wasn't there already.

I quit drinking and started reading books. With no plan at first. I read *Great Expectations* and *Tilly Trotter Wed* and then formulated the idea of learning, of maybe even going to college or university.

'What are you going to study?' asked Julia one afternoon over the blare of the slightly out of tune radio that she never switched off. Like me, she didn't really take the idea that seriously.

I didn't think about it, I just kept on reading.

'English,' I said, lighting up another of her cigarettes.

'I wouldn't mind you smoking all my fags if you smoked them properly,' she said, 'but you don't inhale. Do this,' she said, sucking on her cigarette with such force that her cheeks almost caved in, and the little cloud of white smoke shot into her throat, forcing her to bark it back out again.

Her eyes were still watering when I made my first serious attempt. I took a deep gulp and my heart and brain seemed to rise up an inch or two and in that moment I became a lifelong smoker.

You know, it was going well my old life. But there was one big snag. I seemed to be going out with Jocky. Every time I went anywhere he turned up too and, just when I couldn't stand sitting in the house a minute longer, he'd be at the door and he'd be seriously welcome. My mum thought he was adorable for some reason. When he came squirming to our door, tugging at his sweater cuffs, she'd invite him in and make tea in the teapot and her voice became quasi-posh.

I wouldn't have minded but I just didn't fancy him at all. He was big and he smiled constantly and smelled of wood. All nice things, but on him they depressed me.

He would sit beside me in the pub and grin expectantly whenever I talked and laugh about my smoking which quickly became a standing joke because I did so much of it.

He even bought me books and they were good choices. Oh, it was a lot of Dickens and Jane Austen and predictable stuff like that but it was good of him and he really tried hard to be a good boyfriend.

Only I didn't want him.

Everyone was very pleased about it and that breathed life into it. Julia kept remarking that she could hear the sound of wedding bells and his ears seemed to prick up like a golden retriever's after spotting a bouncy tennis ball and it made me feel awful. Then again, she wasn't saying it for my benefit, or even for Jocky's. It was all for Bob – who would sit there grinning like a sunburned potato – in the hope it would inspire him to want to hear wedding bells playing his tune. But of course it didn't – he had a good bit of farm coming to him, didn't he?

*   *   *

26

I also began to save money. That was easy because, in his capacity as my boyfriend, Jocky paid for everything, including my cigarettes. It was kind of the duty of guys round there to do that. God knows what the single men did with all their wonga. Maybe that's why they were alcoholics.

I siphoned off dribs and drabs of my wages and all my tips, not that they were in any way magnificent, and I began to amass funds. Only a hundred and fifty pounds or so but it was something.

There were no plans for that money as yet, but I knew they were coming.

He usually gave me a kiss at the end of the night. That makes it sound much more gallant than it actually was. Jocky lunged at me when he thought the going was good. Maybe I was actually talking to him or even, when I'd had a lot to drink, leaning into him. I never got used to it and I'd bat him off like he was a randy Labrador, which he seemed to find funny. Not all the time, mind you. He wasn't averse to stumping off down the road when he sensed something of the icy disdain I felt for him.

Poor Jocky. Like I said, he was a lovely guy, he really was. I just couldn't bear him touching me and I really couldn't stand it when David gave him the thumbs up in that matey way of his every time he saw us together.

Maybe that was at the root of it. David just seemed so damned glad to be rid of me.

If anyone had cared to calculate Jocky Gunn's biorhythms at that time of his life, they would have found them to be deeply depressed in all areas, barring his health. The unfortunate lad was in rude, bouncing health throughout his unrequited youth. Come hell or high water, he never missed a meal and always managed to roll out of bed in the morning to perform the menial tasks that comprised his career. Not that I was ever there, of course, but I'm sure he was ruddy even at the dead of night.

His emotional curve, however, must have been skidding along rock bottom. Not only did he have a girlfriend who shuddered when he touched her, he was also written off by all the other girls on account of his being 'attached'.

And his career, which had been nose-diving since he failed his O Grade Arithmetic, was now in freefall. He showed me his report card from school once, during a rare moment of tenderness when I actually agreed to come in for a coffee. The teacher had written, under all his Smiffy of the Bash Street Kids-style grades, that John was 'a likeable lad'.

He gave me a sweet little smile and I almost wept. How terrible. To be summed up as nothing more than 'a likeable lad'.

I had to end this dismal charade of a relationship and this time it wasn't me left standing by the roadside treading dirt. I went and slept with Charlie, didn't I?

6

I wonder what you see when I talk about Charlie. A face as lined as an Ordnance Survey map, with sunburn nestling in the crinkles? An old geezer with a cackle and bow legs? That's what I saw when I first caught him in my peripheral vision; some old guy. But then things happened and he became different, his features became softer and, I don't know, he was warm and brown and there were silver-grey streaks in his hair that rose and fell when he ran his hands through it, so they looked like foam caps being swallowed and regurgitated by the sea. And I wondered how I could have failed to notice this before.

I find it hard to see him the way I saw him then. I laughed about him to myself and, for a little while, to everyone else who'd listen – and there were plenty of them. Ageism was as rife where we lived as racism in apartheid South Africa.

'Kill Piggy! Kill Piggy!' their screwed up eyes squealed when I stuck the knife into the man I'd gone to bed with a week before.

The young men didn't like one of their girls being taken by the older crowd. It made them nervous because it made them aware that youth wasn't enough to distinguish them from the human wreckage around them.

A life spent making money to spend in hotel bars with preposterously vague closing times wasn't enough.

Nor was a bit of farm coming to you or a motorbike you could afford to crash into a dyke.

Before you knew it you too would be chugging off to Naples

29

every summer to live out your sun-faded fantasy of being a watercolourist.

The day after it happened, Julia met me walking through the village with a pint of milk. It was dark and my mouth was oily with the aftertaste of brandy. I felt very odd, emotionally speaking. As if on the verge of discovering something very, very sad but deeply important.

'No Charlie?' she asked, without so much as a smile.

'No.'

I resisted the impulse to shudder ostentatiously and start making a joke of it all. Unfortunately, that thin skin of dignity peeled away pretty quickly.

She took my arm, which was an odd thing for her to do, and walked me all the way home, where she made me a cup of tea so weak it tasted like tears and milk.

I asked her if I should go and see Jocky and she shook her head.

'Don't bother about him,' she said, which was an odd thing for her to say.

In fact, all the next week, when I was saying he was old and I must be mad and everyone else was cheering me on, I kept catching her eye. She didn't think it was funny and I realised later that she was much smarter in this matter than I.

It didn't happen the way you'd imagine. We weren't drunk at some party or ill-met by moonlight after a night in the Drumclair. It happened in the evening when I was walking home from work.

It was very dark and my breath was bellowing from my lungs like the steam from a boiler. It was a dank darkness, everything seemed to be dripping and the road was covered in a thin, watery slush.

My woollen gloves were soaking wet because the water from the urn had seeped into them and my hands felt red and cold. I wanted to be warm but I didn't want to go home because the thought of talking to Mum was too exasperating.

I meandered along the road until I realised I'd passed the entrance to the park but I kept on for a bit anyway.

Then I passed the old cottage by the roadside that the post-master, who'd hanged himself two years before, had lived in. There was a light on in the main room and I remembered that it had been let recently. To Charlie.

It seemed like a good idea to go up and rap on the door. I remember thinking, very clearly, when I heard the inner door open and footsteps approach – 'That's my Charlie.'

He laughed when he saw me. Not at me, but because he was so pleased to see me. I could tell; it seemed to warm up the hallway, which was dark and shadowy but vivid with the smell of new emulsion paint.

'I'm trying to make it not look like the house of a suicide,' he said, taking a jar of coffee out of a blue-painted cupboard. Through the back kitchen window I could see the shadows of the rowan trees swishing in the wind.

On the wall was a poster from the Spanish tourist board. Espana against a Miro sun. It gave off heat.

Charlie smiled at me when he gave me my coffee and his teeth were yellowy white, not yellow, and his eyes were very clear and slate grey.

The lines around them fascinated me and I wanted to touch them. Most of all I wanted to touch his hands, which were very brown and long-fingered.

He made me feel that everything would be just fine. He gave off an air of having done it all before, and it was an air I found very reassuring.

I was sitting on the table, with my coffee cup beside me, when he put his arms round my waist and interlocked his fingers in the small of my back.

He kissed me so softly I barely felt it but my scalp tingled.

A voice in my head was wondering, idly, what this would be like, while the rest of me just let it happen. I was amazed at him and at me, that we were doing this. Maybe he was too.

He led me upstairs by the hand and I sat on the bed unlacing my boots while he sat behind me, lifting my jumper and kissing my back.

I think I might be in danger of making this encounter sound

like a scene from *The Stud*. It wasn't. There was a deal of fumbling and those embarrassing noises that make you flush dark red when you hear them for the first thirty or so times.

But it was as near to *The Stud* as I'd ever been and, in the end, I wanted to do nothing so much as hug him. He was warm and his skin was a satisfyingly sallow brown all over, not red and white like David's.

I also wanted to hug him because I couldn't look him in the eye. I didn't know what to think about it all.

We lay back in his bed for a while afterwards. I heard shouting in the road outside and recognised one of the voices as Jocky's. What the hell was he doing there? I had this awful picture in my mind of him bursting in on us, but the voices seemed to pass.

Then Charlie suddenly bolted upright.

'Christ, I . . . oh Jesus.'

I looked at him and he was almost ashen.

'Jocky's here for the night.'

I thought, well, he won't come upstairs but then, he didn't need to. I'd still have to go down.

We scrambled into our clothes, not looking at each other, and when we got downstairs, Jocky was sitting at the kitchen table. His lip was so petted I nearly burst out laughing but I was also very shocked.

And in the true spirit of courage, I took to my heels and ran all the way home.

Where there was a bottle of brandy and a note from Mum saying she'd be home in the morning, have a drink.

Like I said, I wasn't overly pleasant about Charlie for the rest of the week. He didn't deserve that. He even did a rather good job of talking to Jocky, who came to tell me pompously that I was obviously confused about my feelings and should let him know when he was wanted.

He added, with a note of sarcasm that I hadn't thought him capable of, that Charlie would be charmed to know how ludicrous I found him.

32

I smirked unbecomingly and went back to work feeling deeply, wretchedly confused.

Like the man said, I had no idea what I was doing.

A day or so later I began to get an ache in my gut, an emotional kind of pain like you get with periods.

'What's troubling you?' my mum asked, finding me lying on my bed at eight o'clock in the evening with the lights off.

The truth was that I felt guilty. I was sick with it. Not about Jocky, but about Charlie. I kept thinking about his hand on my stomach and the way he looked at me as if he'd been longing to touch me all his life.

I suddenly couldn't stand it and bounded off the bed in front of my amazed mother, telling her I needed to go out.

She stood aside to let me leave and then ran after me with an army jacket which she threw over my shoulders.

I ran all the way to the main road and then slowed down because I didn't want to be too out of breath when I got there, and then raced down to his door.

He was out, God damn him. He could very well be at the pub and I couldn't stand here waiting till he got back because it would be hours yet and it was freezing.

But I did. I waited and waited, without thinking about what could possibly happen. I waited as other men passed along the road, smoking the last of their fags and grousing about the weather.

I waited as the last bus sailed by sending up showers of water from the puddles. I waited until he finally arrived, shambling up the road by himself.

When he saw me he wasn't sure who I was because of the darkness. When he did his face changed. The laughter was gone and it now almost quivered with dislike.

'What the fuck do you want? Another shag to laugh about down the pub with your friends?'

I mumbled piteously that I'd come to say sorry and he made a nasty, grunting sound.

'And so you fucking should. If you'll excuse me.'

And with that he let himself in and slammed the door in my face.

7

There followed a very bad time.
        I had this idea that I was in love with Charlie and that he would never speak to me again. Every night I would lie awake thinking about him like a lovesick teenager. I suppose I was a lovesick teenager.

That one sexual encounter suddenly glowed like a jewel against the dull cloth of my life. Certainly I wanted him more than I'd ever wanted anyone in my life – so much so that I wanted to assault people for not being him – and I had, without doubt, deeply offended him.

But there was some respite. The fact that he'd told me where to stick it, in his post-pub slur, fired my outrage from time to time. I wouldn't always want to run down to his house and throw myself at him – sometimes I wanted to throw a brick at him.

Moody old bastard.

Jocky was vile. He didn't exactly make a point of coming into the café. He just seemed to be in it all the time, muttering about the smell.

To be fair, he became terribly flustered when he did this. Being a swine wasn't Jocky's way of doing things. He'd much rather be buying rounds and patting people's backs. Well, apart from mine.

I avoided social gatherings of all kinds. Even girls' nights out. I hated meeting Jocky when he'd packed away a series of heavies and wanted to shout and cry at me like a washed up seal. The worst of it was that he had really liked me and would forgive me anything.

I also hated everyone's blatant curiosity about what had happened with Charlie. Had I really gone to bed with him? Had I really gone to the house after slagging him off?

God, I wished I'd handled it all better.

Naturally I told my mother absolutely nothing.

She had been there when I came home that night from Charlie's. I must have looked like someone who'd just had a seizure. I mean, I didn't know how to play a man or anything but I'd never, not ever, been quite so forcefully repelled by one.

This was the second time I'd been given my jotters, emotionally speaking, in six months for God's sake.

The rain streamed onto the chalet floor and instead of the usual clucking sound she made at the sight of mess, Mum just plugged in the kettle and pulled my sodden army jacket from my shoulders.

'You look cold,' she simply said.

I nodded and burst into tears without explaining myself.

She buttered a lot of toast which neither of us ate and lit cigarettes that kept going out. We didn't know how to talk to each other. Sometimes I really wanted to but when I tried she would respond with something so fantastically irritating that I had to stop myself from choking her.

'The ones who're worth it come back,' she said into the pool of silence.

That wasn't too bad. She could have said that I was better off without boys and should be having fun. (What? Without boys?)

If we'd been a different mother and daughter we might have held hands or hugged. Instead, we sat across from each other at the table without saying anything. We just looked at leaflets I'd picked up from the bank and contemplated Savings Bonds.

Going to bed that night was like pressing the button that would make the world end. I thought that was the worst I could possibly feel. How wrong was I?

* * *

The days got shorter and darker. The frosts arrived and I slithered along knuckle-hard road surfaces in pathetically sole-worn boots to get to work – and home again – every day.

I stopped looking out for Charlie after two weeks and began to assume he'd emigrated in order to get away from me. Perhaps he would return with the spring and run full-pelt to my door, tears in his eyes. Perhaps he would just enjoy the Australian sunshine and not give a shit.

I caught a cold in early December that refused to budge. By the time I went to bed it would seem to have cleared and the next morning I'd wake up with my nose glued to the pillow.

Mary and Lea kept trying to send me home. Taking their reiterations for concern rather than for what they were – that is, something to say – I phoned in sick one morning. Only to be greeted with ill-concealed annoyance and a litany of all the things they would have to do in my absence. I'd no idea they thought I worked so hard.

I only took the one day, not because of Mary and Lea, but because being alone all day with a clogged sinus and a head full of ever-decreasing thoughts was worse than watching someone arranging ilex in an empty Paul Masson wine carafe.

No one came to see me, either in the café or at home. I spent my evenings watching TV. I couldn't even be bothered reading my books. I felt unbearably bad about myself and I couldn't find a way to escape it. I even experimented with nightly brandies but that only made matters worse.

Mum, at that time, was hardly ever home.

It came to the shortest day, or the Solstice as our winter visitors would insist on calling it. Around 20 December, the island's population was swelled by the arrival of long-haired strangers bearing scented candles.

The bar of the Drumclair was so thronged with red beards and knee-length jumpers that it looked like a conference of trolls.

The reason was the tree.

It isn't just Glastonbury that has a flowering thorn – according to legend, the one at the end of our churchyard had one too. This mid-winter flowering had, allegedly, occurred most recently in 1931, and people continued to flock.

The tree in question was unbelievably old. Its dense greenery and gnarled branches made it look like the kind of shrub Bilbo Baggins might care to frolic beneath.

Actually, it had always given me the horrors. Corrie once said that it had moved when I wasn't looking. She said it looked as if it was about to tap me on the shoulder – 'foggin' did, like a foggin' Dr Who monster' were her very words – and I'd never shaken off that initial creepy impression.

Back in 1931 it was a local doctor, quite elderly and merry I should imagine, who claimed the old tree had flourished its charms at him.

Some said it was the light from his torch giving the tree a false impression of springtime that teased it into flowering. That explanation is plausible in the case of Glastonbury, where dozens upon dozens of half-frozen sight-seers crouch together brandishing enough candlepower to boil a Highland loch, but one lone torch could hardly cause such a stir.

Still others said that he was plain mad or in the pay of the local tourist office. His family insist to this day that he said nothing regarding the tree whatsoever but the story stuck tenaciously, like chewing gum to a shoe.

The Solstice seekers never missed it and, despite themselves, nor did the locals. It would have been just too, too much to have missed out on if the damn thing really did give it big flowers one year.

My first Solstice I went down with Corrie. Kids were allowed to go themselves because vegetarian men with long hair and no fixed abode weren't considered dangerous in the 1970s.

We nearly fell asleep in the back seat of her dad's old car, the one he'd taken the wheels off and left for dead in front of his kitchen window. He'd left blankets in there specifically for us, or the dogs, to slumber in when it all became too much.

It was ten to midnight when we woke up, gaping as little girls do when startled. We bombed along the main road to the church where a sprawl of silent people were drawing towards the thorn tree. It looked even more witchy and arthritic by candlelight. It looked like a topiary crab showing off.

Everyone waited in dead silence and I honestly don't think I've ever been so excited. Corrie turned to me and she looked like one of those kids you see in adverts for Kinder Egg, the ones who're so excited about their free toy they can't shut their mouths.

She gripped my hand and we stood there, waiting for a miracle.

The church bell rang out at midnight and there was a sigh. Which changed direction suddenly and became a gasp as snow began to fall in the echo of the first bell. It drifted in tiny feathers over the shabby stones, darted into eyes and hissed as it flew into candle-flames.

The minister, at that time a young man called Mr Robertson, came out from the church and invited everyone in for hot chocolate. Corrie and I stayed out until well after two o'clock and both got our bottoms smacked by our respective mothers.

But it was magic nonetheless.

I hadn't missed it since, even though it usually entailed going with my mum, who claimed to be afraid of the dark and seemed to be deaf to all bad-tempered entreaties to bloody well stay in then.

I couldn't miss it this year. That would have been too desperately awful. But I couldn't go with anyone because I was too sad and ashamed. In the end I walked down with Mum, who chainsmoked in the dark and occasionally clutched my arm to let me know that she was still there and still caring.

The sky was totally black that night. There must have been cloud cover but it felt very claustrophobic, like we were being pressed down into our button of earth.

The light from the candles, there must have been fifty, maybe a hundred, barely pierced the gloom. We perched on the slope leading up to the tree, next to a drunkenly skewhiff headstone covered in ivy. In the false light the leaves were very vivid and green.

The shadow of people moving around in the flickering light made me think of nocturnal scenes-of-crime. All it needed was a yard or two of tickertape and a flashing blue light.

Somehow, due to the ebbing and flowing of the crowd, we found ourselves at the frontline. For the first time I stood in the inner ring of thorn tree watchers – and I didn't even have a candle. We'd used our last when the meter ran out the night before.

Looking up at the unperforming tree I sensed someone watching me and looked down to see Charlie. He looked cold and nasty but he nodded in my direction. Involuntarily I waved, like the Queen Mum from her carriage. Tra-la-la, I waved.

And he waved back, just as unthinkingly girlishly, and smiled for a second. It was just long enough for me to imagine I detected warmth.

Beside him stood David and Lorraine. She wore a thick white jumper riddled with complex ribbing and multi-coloured patches of embroidery. He looked as if he'd been hit over the head with a club, which meant he was probably half-cut. She looked at him and her eyebrows contracted slightly in annoyance and then her expression cleared and she snaked an arm around his waist. I would never have dared but he seemed either not to notice or not to mind.

Behind them stood Julia and Bob. Bob kept tapping people's shoulders or nudging them. As if anything was better than being left with only his girlfriend to talk to. She always smiled though, as if she found these constant slights amusing.

She was swathed in a giant, quilted coat her mum liked her to wear. It made her look like a sleeping bag with legs but she never refused because she always did what her mum wanted. Her mum said that she and Julia were more like friends than family, but I was never convinced and I don't think Julia was either. She could have found better friends than that.

Or maybe not. Suzanna, having acquired a boyfriend, had receded from our little triangle of friendship. I thought it was just me she never bothered to call round for any more but, judging by how far away she stood from Julia in the graveyard, Miss Donald had clearly been dismissed too. Tucking her boyfriend's hand into the back pocket of her snow-washed denims, Suzanna scanned the crowd blankly, failing to register much more than a blip when her gaze encountered mine.

Everyone else was a stranger to me apart from the new minister, an old man called David Honeyman, who stood there with us, his fiery eyes fixed on the thorn as if it were the very gate of hell itself.

And then the bell tolled and we all let out the annual sigh, followed by a laugh. It was such a ritual, that sigh, that even the visitors joined in.

The children and elderly trooped into the church for hot chocolate and as many mince pies as they could get into their pockets, while the rest stampeded to the Drumclair for last orders.

Mum wanted brandy but she didn't want to go to the pub so I went in to buy a half bottle while she prowled outside, boosting the profits of Benson and Hedges.

'Your mum's out there,' said everyone who came in after me and I nodded wearily.

It was like Christmas Eve really. It was our dry, or not so dry, run. I ordered a bottle of something revolting and cheap – it would be fine in coffee – and watched everyone being served lovely pints of beer while I waited. I could have murdered for the opportunity to stay out boozing but the only way was to walk Mum all the way home and come back again. Which meant both of us being alone, because nobody wanted me anyway.

As I thought this I felt Charlie's breath on the back of my neck. He kissed my ear and said, 'But I want you.' Or at least, I think he did.

I turned and he smiled at me.

'Your mum's out there,' he said.

'I know, I know. I put her there.'

I got my brandy, in a festive Presto bag, and he followed me.

'I'll walk you home,' he said, and he did. We ambled along in near silence.

Charlie made a few stabs at small talk, as did I, while Mum made surreptitious eye-rolling motions at me.

'You must talk to me soon,' said Charlie, just before he said goodbye.

8

Twelve hours later I was sitting at the table surveying the bleak vision of the chalet park being battered by a gale. In front of me was a list of things we needed to get through what we laughingly referred to as the Festive Season.

'And potatoes. The wee ones,' said my mother as she searched the cupboards one more time hoping, perhaps, for the Atora suet to turn into a plum pudding.

I absolutely hated Christmas. For us it was like the aftermath of a nuclear holocaust. We saw nobody, we ate things from tins and the TV reception went scratchy on account of the freak weather conditions. Every year I wondered if our dinky little home would end up on its side and, quite frankly, I wouldn't have cared if it had. At least the firemen who came to cut us out the wreckage would have been a bit of company.

It always began with the list of things we neither had the facilities to cook nor the transport to bring home. Then there was the long, arduous trip to the supermarket, at which we generally arrived ten minutes before closing time on Christmas Eve, and the harrowing journey back.

We were arguing about the potatoes when there was a knock at the door. Such was our general mood that I half expected to open up and find the Grim Reaper standing there, sherry in hand. What was there was even more of a shock really. It was a dead pheasant with a note pinned to its unfortunate little breast.

'Merry Christmas Folks!' it read, signed with an F.

As I gazed at the sagging beast my mum swept it up in her arms like it was a bouquet of lilies and smiled knowingly at me.

'Is this from . . . ?' I began and she nodded.

'But it's a fucking pheasant. How are we going to cook a fucking pheasant without an oven? And who's going to get all those feathers off?'

She fixed me with her wise old look, wrapped Frankie's pheasant in several sheets of newspaper and handed it to me with a satisfied smile.

'Ask Mary to cook it,' she said. 'Tell her that's one I owe her. And get carrots too. They go nice with bird.'

Mary and my mother went back a long way. Just after we moved here they had a spectacular spat in the café about how much turkey should be put in a roll.

Mary said my mother had outrageous manners and my mum said Mary was a stingy old tart. It had nearly come to slaps when a pensioner intervened and got his cap knocked off.

It made me very popular at school for days afterwards and it established a never to be broken bond between the two of them. Every day Mary asked after my mother and every fortnight or so my mother sent me down to beg a favour, with the promise of one in return. No such returned favours ever came to pass but then, Mary never asked.

Mary was the sort of woman who would rather die in a ditch than ask for a hand to get out of it. Self-sufficient and broad, she battled through life like an ox that imagined itself a holy martyr.

As expected, she took the pheasant with a smile and set to work divesting it of its entrails before a full house of startled tea-drinkers.

Outside I saw Frank McAllister sweep past in his Land Rover with an expression on his face that suggested Satan and his legion of assistants were on his tail.

And as I marched purposefully round and round the single aisle of the Spar, searching for carrots and tinned pudding, I tried to imagine what would be waiting for him at home.

I pictured his wife as thin and wan, with a passion for planting pansies and stone animals in her garden. Their sons would be three scowling versions of Peter Phillips, all dedicated to the art of firing air-guns at people's dogs and making Airfix models.

He would slope in, his wax jacket stained with the blood of game, and eat Baxter's soup by himself in the kitchen while everyone else ignored him. And then, after imbibing a whole bottle of Drambuie on Christmas morning, his wife would rail at him for making her life a living hell while he grabbed her spindly wrists and told her to take a Valium. His rusty red eyes would glare as she struggled helplessly, spitting at him through her teeth. Then would come the kerrrack! as her wrists snapped and her eyes popped out their sockets and rolled along the Persian rug like two bloody marbles . . . and there it was, the last of the Christmas puddings, and a non-alcoholic one at that.

Mary told me she would take the pheasant up to my mother herself so I quickly crunched up the road to the house to warn her that a social life of sorts was imminent.

This news transformed my mother from reclining *Take A Break* reader to whirling dervish after the manner of Valerie Singleton. I had never before seen paper chains so speedily attached to chalet ceilings as artificial trees the size of cornettos sprang up in clearings on the shelves.

I left her to it. I'd not thought about Charlie all day. It felt like I'd been holding my breath for hours as I clambered out the door.

Almost at the road I realised I was still wearing the jeans and jumper I'd put on first thing and I about-turned abruptly. I needed a shower and to wash my hair. I needed something clean to wear and some mascara. I actually needn't have bothered but, back then, I didn't realise that Charlie and shower gel were strangers to each other.

I met him just as he was locking his door.

'Do you want me to go?' I asked, because I suddenly had this feeling he might swear at me again.

'Of course not,' he laughed and turned to unlock the door again. His hand was trembling a little bit and the key slipped the first time.

43

'Were you going somewhere?' I asked.

'Nowhere important. I can't sit around and wait for you all the time.'

I was shrugging and trying to think of a response when he pushed me in the door.

The kitchen was as I remembered it, except that no one had washed any dishes since my last visit. The Miro sun looked a little less bright. But then, it had recently witnessed scenes of intense intra-familial strife.

Charlie shrugged at the bonfire of cutlery and glasses. 'I know, I don't always housekeep that well.'

I noticed that his hair was very greasy as he leaned over to pull the cork out of a bottle of wine. Oddly enough it didn't put me off him. These things happened. Guys didn't care.

He handed me a glass of cold red wine and a lit cigarette.

'Have I ruined your life?' I joked.

He laughed. 'What a young thing to say.'

I hated that. Idiot. I was only fucking joking.

He sat down at the table but I stayed standing. He held out his hand.

'Give me your hand. Please.'

So I did and I told him I was sorry. He shooed my words away, saying it didn't matter, that what did he expect, I was young enough to be his daughter.

I found this a rather annoying thing of him to say and said so. We niggled at each other and finished the bottle and opened another.

Charlie was very thin. You didn't notice most of the time, but when he stood beside a bevy of farm boys you noticed that all his bones were prominent and his jeans hung loosely on his waist.

I noticed that night as his hands toyed with the stem of his glass. His wristbones emerging and submerging under his skin. I liked his skin, it was brown and smooth and it made you want to touch it.

He never got back to the subject of why I'd said all those things about him. Instead we talked about all the places in America we wanted to visit.

44

It was rather good. I never got the chance to smoke and drink with men who wanted to talk to me. I felt like an actress in a *Screen Two* production; something difficult about love. In character I walked to the window and looked out. There was a bright moon shaped like a thumbnail. There were even a few stars.

'I'll take you home,' he said at my shoulder. He took a puff of his cigarette and looked at me like a dealer eyeing up a horse: completely dispassionate, completely frank.

I found it wildly sexy but I didn't ask to stay. Apart from anything else I was too pissed.

'Let's go out for dinner, just you and me. You know, a date.'

I told him I couldn't leave Mum on her own over the next two days and he said, in that case, it could wait till Boxing Day.

'Plenty of time,' he said, in his easy way.

Before we reached my door he put his arm around my neck and kissed me. I mean a real kiss, like he'd kissed me while his hand held my thigh against his waist and a trickle of sweat ran down behind my ear.

In the bright light of the chalet I helped my mother, who was in exuberant spirits, repair the many tears in the paper chains.

They dipped so low across the table I worried they might constitute a fire hazard. After all, there were two smokers in the house this year.

My face and neck tingled, like someone had been tickling it for hours with a feather and finally left off. I wondered what Charlie was doing. He told me later he'd been washing dishes.

9

I won't bore you with the details of our Yuletide celebrations. We were holed up for the traditional forty-eight hours but, unlike other years, I was terribly happy.

Mum was too, in a dazed kind of way. She sipped white wine on an almost constant basis and repeated, time and again, things Mary had said. Things like, 'If this is the eighties boom, I want to know when I'm getting my share.' Or, 'I don't see what all the fuss is about Anne Diamond, but I wouldn't mind having her money.'

Really, she should have been on the stage.

Because we didn't have a phone I was saved all the usual teenage angst of waiting for it to ring. I just had to assume that, were Charlie getting legless at a party somewhere, no one would touch him with a barge-pole. It was rather comforting to be attracted to someone that nobody else fancied.

I dreamt on Christmas Night that he lived with us and slept with my mother. As they sprawled on her bed, he asked me to make his toast the way he liked it. But as I waited for the toast to pop up out the toaster I noticed that the whole chalet was ankle deep in water and five pound notes were streaming out the door like leaves straining from a corner of a guttering.

I woke up with my tongue glued to the roof of my mouth and my stomach churning. Vowing to give up drinking for a week I suddenly realised that it was Boxing Day which meant my exile was over. Which meant I would soon see Charlie.

*   *   *

He came to the door in the late afternoon and said what about eight o'clock? He flinched under my mother's steely gaze.

'I don't like him,' she said, unnecessarily, once he was gone.

'Don't go out with him then,' I muttered as I turned on the shower.

My face looked like it was made of bread dough. Bread dough pocked with three glacé cherries, two of which were on my chin.

As I leaned into the mirror, my two index finger nails kneading furiously at these unsightly presences, I realised that my Xmas internment had not only made me spotty. It had also made me heavy. Or hefty as I used to phrase it when I was an unselfconscious (and round) little girl.

'I'm hefty!' I would announce adorably to passers-by as I wedged another bourbon biscuit into my hamster-like cheek.

Now it didn't seem so cute. I might as well not have bothered with my diet at all. Two months of baked potatoes spoiled by two days – alright, two or three weeks – of eating like an unhappy schoolboy. I wondered what the hell I was going to wear. I didn't have a very extensive wardrobe and what there was of it only just fitted anyway.

And we were going for dinner, so it wasn't like I could even calm myself with the fancy that this was the first day of a new diet and my weight was on its way down. I felt like shooting myself by the time I got those spots squeezed, I really felt awful and it made me argumentative.

'So why don't you like him?' I demanded of Mum as I emerged from the sauna-like bathroom, great bales of steam rising from my head.

'He's too old for you,' she said. 'I liked Jocky. He was better for you.'

'Why? Why was he better? Because he was twenty-five, not . . . ehm . . . because he was in his twenties?' Actually I had no idea what age Charlie was.

My mother's nostrils flared as she exuded two long flutes of smoke. She turned to gaze out the window. A fine romantic gesture marred only by the fact that it was pitch dark out there.

I could either cajole her into a semi-good mood or ignore her.

I chose the latter and went to find something to wear. I tried on everything I owned, knowing full well that I would end up in the black shift dress I wore for everything but work and which smelled faintly of the last time I doused it with perfume as a substitute for washing it.

Seven cigarettes, two stripes of black kohl, one dose of red lipstick and a cloud of toxic hairspray went into making me as presentable as I could possibly be. A stone less of bodymass and a new dress would have finished the job nicely but I did the best I could.

My room reeked of nasty chemicals and fags by the time my mother pushed open the door and told me she could hear him approaching.

She gave me a sideways look as she sniffily opened my window onto the bitter night, her cigarette wedged in the side of her mouth.

'You look nice,' she said, practically vomiting up the stub, 'Will you be back tonight?'

'No.' And Charlie rapped on the door.

He drove me to a hotel on the other side of the island. The car was one he was fixing for someone, but that was pretty much the norm round here. The guy probably wouldn't have thought twice about it had he known.

The hotel was set back from the road and surrounded by bony, naked trees. I thought we were just on some long, bendy backroad when we suddenly swerved round a curve and drew up in front of a black shoulder of house. Every window glowed with yellow light and the glossy white doors stood open to the night.

The candles that guttered frenziedly on the edge of the steps reflected in the paintwork like the whirling wings of tropical butterflies.

'I never knew about this,' I said. I was astonished at how beautiful it was, how it could be here in our backwater of abandoned tyres and rotting carpets left in outhouses. 'Do you, have you been here before?'

'Only once for dinner, but I've worked here on and off for

years. It's a great place, it's where the film crews stay when they come over to shoot ads for stout.'

He bounded up the steps in front of me and the door was opened by a man he mockingly called Sir. Sir laughed a single yip and called him Charles.

The staff liked him which pleased me enormously. It made me feel more secure about liking him myself. I wasn't what you might call a free spirit in those days; it mattered very much what the world thought.

He ordered a bottle of wine so thickly red it took ages to drink it. It was a bit like sucking on a velvet curtain.

Charlie looked good. He'd washed his hair so it looked like he had a lot more of it. His suit was slightly shabby and it had a shiny patch where he must have, at one time, tried to iron out a crease. I clearly wasn't the only one who had struggled to look half-decent.

We smoked cigarettes as we tussled with menus the size of place-settings.

A few did I want a starter, what are you having and oh, if you think so, and you firsts later, we had ordered soup that was so thick you could have stood a spoon up in it, and chicken embedded in a landscape of rough-cut vegetables.

I was captivated by it all. I loved the texture and colour. I loved the bruised blue paint on the walls and the crackling flaws in the plasterwork. And the violent outlines of the thistles that stood starkly upright in their tall glass vases.

It was so expensively modern; the sort of place you'd get in London. Not my Dad's mini-cab London of shabby terraces and arid parks, but that place inhabited by former models who thought having lunch was an occupation.

All we had on the island were the relics of the seventies, when the poorer end of society had apparently done all its decorating. They'd gone mad with swirly lampshades and hessian wallpaper, nailing it down in hotels, fun emporiums and B&Bs until all the money ran out and they had to live with it for eternity.

Here, flickering oil lamps and candles made everything soft and luxurious, even our harsh features and crude clothes.

Charlie told me four times that I looked beautiful, and I didn't believe it but I made a start on the path toward believing it. I had even stopped thinking about how much weight I'd put on and instead thought about Charlie's body and what his chest and shoulders would look like if he were naked in this light.

Maybe he was thinking the same about me.

Dreamily I asked him, 'How old are you Charlie?'

The next instant it was as if the film score had come to a sudden, twanging stop. He looked at me as if I'd just chopped his thumb off and eaten it.

'Forty-four.'

Oh. Deep down I had hoped he was just a bit younger.

'I'm eighteen.'

'I know. Is it a problem, do you think?'

'It's twenty-six years.'

My brain got out its calculator and whizzed through some sums. He'd be sixty-six when I was forty. That was OK. But I'd only be twenty-two when he was fifty. Our kids would have a near pensionable dad if I waited till thirty to have them.

But I might have no kids at all. And die at thirty-one. And there was Humphrey Bogart and Lauren Bacall.

'No, it doesn't feel like it's a problem. You get couples who have that. Like Lauren Bacall and Humphrey Bogart.'

He smiled and looked down at his chest. 'So there was. Well, that's alright then.'

Then he clinked my glass and gave me a dirty wink.

'It's alright. You don't have to marry me just because I took you out to dinner. We'll see how it goes, will we?'

My heart sank a little. I suppose he was just being cautious but I felt like men had been cautious with me all my life. And I said so.

He worked hard at not laughing and then said, 'OK, fuck that. Marry me.'

'Och Charlie.'

'Go on.'

'Stop it!'

I remember the light from the headlights blanching the trees as we passed and the sound of the wind rattling at my window, which was faulty apparently.

Charlie poured us a Bell's to keep out the chill but we didn't drink it straightaway because we fell onto the living-room floor and made love there instead of in the bed upstairs. Simply because we could.

Last thing we scampered up the stairs, half freezing to death. I finished my whisky, listening to a storm whip up outside while Charlie smoked a fag in the dark with one hand and stroked my hair with the other.

10

The days between Christmas and New Year are like dead wood. Even now, with enough experience to know better, I look forward to the last days of the year as the great kick-back season of long walks in the cold air and books and wine. And every year I'm bewildered by the way it ends up.

Two weeks of treading water, waiting to flip over the calendar and move on. Waiting to stop drinking and having hangovers and visitors.

One year I had flu and spent the entire time in bed reading books by South American writers. Thanks to my huge intake of flu remedies and the occasional glass of red wine I lived in a fug of blurry senses and surreal images. It was quite the best Christmas of all. I even missed New Year.

Another time I worked right through and ate sandwiches with my boss when the bells came in. He simpered at me sweetly and paid for my taxi home through a city so quiet you'd think a biological weapon had hit it.

The others were all muddy, slightly indigestible wastes of time.

The only exception to this rule being the first round of dead wood days I spent with Charlie.

Everything from tea to dustbins had a previously unseen charm. Everything was sharp and unique.

The world had altered, as if a new government had come to power, or I had woken up in the body and life of someone much better than me.

My consciousness was so heightened I could have heard ships on the Solent.

Sometimes I just closed my eyes and pictured his arms emerging too soon from the sleeves of his black suit jacket, which was way too small for him. In my mind he was always sitting forward, his wrists on his knees, looking up at me as he listened. Once in a while he would scratch at his hair like a dog at a flea.

He woke me up on the 27th with a cup of tea which he sat and watched me drink.

'Good morning?' I said quizzically.

'I can't believe you're here,' he said.

'Well, I hate to say I told you so, but you did plan it this way.'

'I know. It's good, isn't it?'

We didn't leave his house until mid-afternoon when it was already getting dark. We walked up to the chalet park, where I belted on the door to warn my mother we were coming in. Unsurprisingly, she was out.

Charlie sat at the edge of the table and gazed at the paper chains in dismay while I got changed into jeans and stuffed clean clothes into a bag.

'You're not staying then?' he asked.

'Oh. What, should I?'

I was used to the idea that, when things were going on, you just packed up your stuff and lived in someone else's house for a while. I used to stay at David's for days on end, even when he wasn't there sometimes because there would be other people. We all just kind of drifted in a gang. But, of course, me and Charlie weren't part of a gang.

I stood there dumbly, an Arran jumper half-way into my army bag.

He looked at me for a second or two before relaxing into a grin.

'Go on then. Don't mind if you do. But leave her a note or something. She doesn't trust me.'

I wrote her a nice note in fact, signed with kisses. I said we'd call in the next night and bring wine, if she liked. Not that she

53

could do anything about it if she didn't like. I couldn't see her slipping her thin feet into her Dunlop Green Flashes and nipping down to Charlie's in the dead of night to leave a note under his mat.

Then we walked all the way down to the sea in the near darkness. I do this in Glasgow, walking down to the river, but you never get away from the haze of the lights and it makes the night murkier. There it was pitch black and wrapped itself around you like a blanket.

Eventually you saw the waves and the pebbles and rocks and Charlie took my hand and held it as we marched nowhere through the freezing air.

The lights from houses on the mainland bobbed above the water like iridescent buoys. They looked lonely and distant. I felt like it must be awful to be anyone other than me.

And then suddenly the sky turned grey and it began to sleet. It was two miles back to Charlie's and neither of us were athletes. We slithered across ditches and fields with the sleet in our eyes but we held hands despite it being a handicap.

His living room was very cold unless the gas heater had been on for at least half an hour. We stood in front of it, shoulder to shoulder, and shivered and bickered about who was to go into the icy kitchen and turn the water heater on.

Charlie gave in and sprinted through, but not before he shook all the rain out of his hair and onto me. I attempted to reciprocate but long hair doesn't shed water quite so effectively and I ended up whipping him across the cheek.

'Ouch!' he yelled, departing. He came back with two tea cups half full of whisky and a blanket which we lay down under.

'Your carpet smells of biscuits,' I remarked.

'I'll get a pillow. My pillows smell like tatties.'

When he came back I'd finished my drink and we had another and I asked him how long he'd been divorced.

'Me and Kate? God, it must be five or six years but we'd been apart for much longer, more like ten.'

'Do you miss her?'

'No. How about David?'

'Oh no, not at all.' I was surprised how dismissive I was about David. Once I'd dusted down my ego I almost completely stopped thinking about him. Even during that tiresome thing with Jocky I didn't make any comparisons in David's favour.

And this with Charlie. It was like comparing Dairylea triangles to a piano concerto. They weren't the same thing at all.

I looked at him as he gazed at the ceiling, his arm slung behind his head. He had a big, full mouth and I thought about the way he kissed me. About his tongue moving into my mouth and the little moan he would sometimes give, deep in his chest. It was more erotic than all my previous experiences put together; it sent electric shocks through to my nerve ends.

'What is it you like about me?'

He sat up on one elbow. 'Your bigness.'

I wondered in horror if he was one of those guys who liked big, rounded ladies – Reubens-style Venuses with six chins. Surely to Christ I wasn't in that category.

He read my expression and laughed.

'You're rolling your eyes like a cow going to slaughter,' he said.

'I thank you.'

'You always stood out from everyone else. I didn't even realise I was doing it but I was always looking out for you.'

'Did you think we would . . . ?'

'No!' And he smiled a long, sentimental smile with his head on one side like a Jack Russell, and even though his eyes didn't move he seemed to be looking at me all over.

Then he said very seriously, 'You're interesting. You're the only person round here who is ever going to do anything worth doing.'

'You're interesting too.'

He shrugged. 'If you say so, but I'm never going to do anything.'

'Don't say that. What would you like to do?'

'For one, I'd like to paint this house. It's the first house I've ever had.'

'Really?'

'Yup. Impressive, eh? But it's going to be a good house.'

'I can feel it. Oh, but what about the postman – doesn't he haunt it?'

'That postie has been bloody good for me. Thanks to him this house was very competitively priced, I can tell you.'

We drank to the dreadful despair of the postman because we were thoughtless beasts who cared for nothing but sex and drink.

Incidentally, we didn't have our baths till morning.

11

He sent me home the next day. I couldn't believe it. I thought he was joking when he said it would be a good idea if I toddled up to the chalet park and spent the night with my mum.

'Why?' I wanted to know as I furiously slathered butter onto toast.

'Because she doesn't trust me. She thinks I'm too old for you and it'll just make her worse if it looks like I've spirited you away to my hovel.'

'She'll never like you, you know. I don't know why you're bothering.'

My heart nearly stopped after I'd said that. Charlie looked at me aghast and I hastily back-pedalled.

'She will eventually, she's just thrawn. She's never liked any of my boyfriends. She doesn't even like my female friends. In fact, I don't think she's ever liked anyone.'

Charlie just looked at me.

'So there.'

'You're still going home for a night, young lady.'

'Won't you miss me?'

'Of course I'll fucking miss you but if we spend every night together then it will seem like such a huge deal if one of us wants to be alone in the future, and it needn't be.'

'Do you want to spend lots of nights without me?'

'For God's sake!'

Maybe he was right. I really needed to go home. I needed something clean to wear and I wanted to shave my legs which was something I didn't feel I could do in front of Charlie.

Mum was in a lively mood when I got back. She was polishing some perfectly hellish porcelain figurine that Frank must have given her. I'd certainly never seen it before.

It was a shepherdess with a waist as narrow as her neck and a dainty little patch of grass on which to rest her obscenely tiny feet. I noted that she had a mate, a wilting fop with lips so full you could have burst them with a pin.

Such was Mum's infatuation with her swooning lovers that she had cleared a spot on the table and laid out a lace napkin to accommodate their respective clods of porcelain earth.

I was horrified and embarrassed. Why did mothers have to fill their living quarters with naff things that visitors might see? Why couldn't they have taste?

It could, of course, be deliberate, something they did to make you wince and thus develop character.

I know I was a terrible tartar about furnishings and fittings when I was a teenager. I just couldn't help it and I believe that those figurines were the first in a succession of factors that finally drove me from under my mother's wing.

But she was pleased to see me that night.

'Hello love,' she said, rubbing away at her maiden's thigh. And, 'I thought we might have wine with tea.'

Wine for tea would have been even better, as I'd determined to make this a low-calorie night, but with was good too.

While Mum cooked omelettes made from everything left in the fridge, I washed all my tops and knickers and painstakingly wrung them out before draping them on a chair in front of the heater.

Unfortunately we both smoked so much that they had no chance of being anything other than impregnated with the smell of cigarettes but at least they would all look clean.

I also did a henna wax treatment on my hair. Applying it and sitting with a damp towel turban was the easy part. Rinsing it out took almost an hour and my hair felt just as rough around the edges as before. But it was exciting. Doing things for someone else's benefit was a better-than-nothing substitute for being with them.

'You like this one, don't you?' Mum asked me as I stood with my head in the shower cubicle, washing henna wax into my eyes.

'Yes.'

'I just think he's too old for you. I worry that he'll hold you back.'

'Mum, let's get this straight. If he even *thinks* he's gonna stop me working my way to the top at that café I'm gonna kill him.'

'Alright,' she said in a withered tone, 'But he'll want you to stay here. He won't want you to go to university or get a job somewhere interesting.'

I found all this stuff infuriating. Charlie may have been older but he wasn't some deadbeat in search of a little wife. And as for my alternatives, well, if anyone would want to pull the shutters down on my horizons it was someone like Jocky, a man who thought it was acceptable to let his mum bring him breakfast in bed every morning. No wonder he had no sex life – who the hell wants to meet their new fella's mother while still naked, streaked in mascara and smelling of KY Jelly?

I didn't mention this. I just muttered about Jocky being a twat while she muttered about Jocky not being my only alternative.

She added, 'You don't read your books any more. You read all the time before.'

Well, if that was all it took to meet with her approval, there was no problem. I took up *Tess of the D'Urbervilles* from where I'd left her and retired to bed. But not before I'd put on an inch-thick layer of Nivea which was intended to give me peachy skin by the morning but mostly ended up greasing the pillow.

It was funny being at home. I'd only been away two nights with Charlie and it felt funny already.

On Hogmanay, Mum did something very strange. She came out to the pub and stayed there for the bells. It was all down to Mary and her oxen resolve. I'd given up trying to spring Mum from her holiday home prison years ago.

Mary arrived, a she-mountain in a surprisingly fabulous black velvet dress, just as I was snipping open two boil-in-the-bag cod in butter sauces. I bolted mine in order to get out of there sharpish or else I would have to suffer my mum's voice become increasingly shrill, as it tended to when she was in the company of someone she hadn't given birth to.

It was nerves. She got herself into a complete state about not boring people or making them think she was common. I had every sympathy, not being the witty life and soul of the nation's social clubs myself, but I couldn't listen to it.

And anyway, the sooner I got out of there, the sooner I'd see Charlie. He said come down anytime and I reckoned it was OK to come down as soon as possible.

While I was gone, Mary got my mother merry on Bailey's Irish Cream and refused to leave for 'the party I wait all year for' unless my mum came too. So there she was, a vision in tight jeans and high heels, clutching a Snowball with both hands and wearing a facial expression last seen when the *Titanic* ran out of lifeboats.

Charlie had his arm round my waist when we walked into the Royal Stuart and I caught Julia's eye the minute we arrived. She sashayed over and said hello. It was the first time I realised that she flirted with all my boyfriends, and that she just assumed they would find her more attractive because she was eight inches shorter and had a bigger chest.

I only really noticed then because I'd never seen anyone flirt with Charlie. And I'd never seen anyone so completely stonewall Julia. He wasn't nasty, he just turned to me and winked but he might as well have slapped her with his fan in full view of the assembled company. She took it quite well, all things considered. At least Charlie bought her a drink.

The bar was alarmingly busy. It always was at this time of year. The other places either shut or looked like Wild West saloons after a major shoot-out. They couldn't compete with the Royal Stuart on Hogmanay simply because no one ever considered the idea of going anywhere else.

As a result it was packed, hot and deafening. This was good from my point of view. I had pictured us walking into a barn of a bar, with everyone sat round a giant table, and them all turning round to stare at us and our clasped hands before clinking their beer glasses and roaring with laughter.

This way, we could just sidle up to people, or be sidled up to, bawl remarks into each other's faces and move on. Bob grinned at us like it was all a big joke, his face swimming in front of us like a giant red flounder.

Jocky nodded and disappeared and David came to the surface, put his arms round us both and said he was fucking sick of women, he was going solo. He eyed me unsteadily, blew me a kiss and was swallowed up by the seething waves of good cheer.

Leandra's husband Mick leaned towards me like a Canadian redwood being felled and planted a bearded kiss on my cheek and Lea followed, circling my neck with her little white hands and telling me she was so happy.

In the intervals we were alone Charlie kissed me, usually on the neck or full on the mouth, very Tommy Lee you might say, but no one could see us amid all that close-packed revelry.

The sea of bodies reached its crescendo at midnight, when arms and legs and heads rose and fell in waves to 'Auld Lang Syne' and elderly men made the most of their annual opportunity to put their tongues into young women's mouths.

We escaped just after I kissed my startled mother, and listened outside in the darkness to the hoarse hee-hawing that counted for singing in our neck of the woods.

We clinked our smuggled out glasses and kissed and laughed.

Charlie wrapped his arms around me and drank his whisky over my shoulder and said that this would be a good year, this was the one.

He pulled my woolly hat, an Army and Navy stores balaclava rolled up, down over my face, said 'That's better' and led me by the hand to the next party. Me looking like an IRA heavy being towed off by my minder.

12

W e seemed to have been together for so long, and almost without meeting a soul too, that I'd kind of forgotten that Charlie didn't exist in a vacuum. That, in point of fact, he knew dozens more people than I did and they were all much nicer to him than any of my friends were to me.

We stopped at someone's husband's brother, a guy called Neil whose larder floor surface was entirely taken up by beautifully washed, empty whisky bottles.

He was one of those men who sports a beard, in his case a bushy black beard, without a moustache, giving him the appearance of a sixteenth-century blacksmith. Except that his sweatshirt invited you to hit him with Your Rhythm Stick.

'How long did that take you?' asked Charlie, nodding at the bottle collection, and Neil shook his head and said 'Oh no' in a very quiet, mournful voice.

His guests, a very thin woman with long grey hair and two men who looked like a cross between her and Neil, sat in his kitchen where the range boomed out heat. After only a few minutes I could feel the pulse in my temple and my cheeks were aflame.

They were a quiet, smiling lot. Actually they were an absolutely sozzled lot.

The woman kept repeating that it was 'good to see Charlie with a woman' and 'good' and 'woman' and Neil told us, in a voice barely above a whisper, that the weather was terrible and he'd rather live in Argyll. At this, his two male relatives nodded vigorously and smiled and said, oh so softly, that they would too.

We left after a dose of Islay malt and a Dubonnet, and made our way to Alec and Moira's. They owned the Drumclair and having bowed to the tradition of the Royal Stuart, now had the night off.

'Aye, but they're good folk, they work hard,' Alec remarked on the matter of his staff – not that I'd asked – as he poured me a gin from a giant optic on his dining-room wall.

I had a memory flash of Charlie leaning over the bar time and time again, talking down to Alec as he fussed over the bottles of mixers in the lower gantry. A sudden flash of Charlie Past, the guy who lived in my peripheral vision and didn't have sex with me. He had lighter hair then, I'm sure of it.

Alec was much the same but as he talked to me I could feel that Alec Past was slipping away too.

He talked to me as if Charlie and I had been a couple for years and blithely issued invitations to dinner on every conceivable occasion you could imagine having dinner.

I didn't know then that these dinners only ever happened when you stumbled home together after a huge drinking binge. At the time I just thought, Christ, if I eat all those dinners I'll end up the size of a house.

'And what about your mother these days, Karen? She's a quiet wee soul, isn't she? Bit like yourself.'

'Oh, she's fine. Quiet. You know.'

Later I was on Charlie's knee in a corner of the settee and we started kissing and ignoring everyone else, which was horribly rude but everyone took it in their stride. Someone's granny, possibly Alec's, stared at us with an alarmed expression on her face. It turned out that she only wanted to know who 'Charlie Boy was having it off with'. She didn't actually mind.

Moira interrupted us with two new gin and tonics.

'You know the fish Old Steely brings from the fish farm? Well, it's got sea lice,' she said.

*   *   *

Later, shambling along the road towards the farm that Bob had coming to him, I said to Charlie, 'You look like Gabriel Byrne.'

He snorted and said, 'No I don't. You're confused because I'm wearing a shabby black suit and Gabriel Byrne sometimes wears a shabby black suit in his fillums.'

'Oh, that's it.'

He stopped to light a cigarette and I had to laugh because he looked like someone in a pantomime pretending to be pissed.

It seemed to take hours to reach the house, probably because it did. Drink didn't exactly make sprinters of us.

Bob's dad, Bob, greeted us with the news that there was plenty of whisky left. I was astonishingly bored of drinking whisky. It made me feel drowsy and heavy and I wanted to be lively and funny. But I drank it nonetheless and Charlie and Bob senior said things to me and to each other and to no one in particular.

As the night grew weary Bob senior leaned forward, put his hand very heavily and solemnly on my knee, and began singing 'Auld Lang Syne'.

My manners must have been standing at some distance from myself because I openly guffawed at him, throwing my head back and showing the room my fillings. But he continued anyway and Charlie, oh Charlie!, joined in and by that time his eyes were so hooded he looked like someone had been boxing with him.

We went to sleep in a bright room with a dark square window beside a long white bed. I kissed Charlie on the cheek. He looked like a drunk priest laid out on a stretcher.

We woke with a bright square window pouring light into our eyes, tussled our way out of our clothes and went back to sleep.

It must have been two o'clock before we made it downstairs. Bobs senior and junior were at the table, shovelling eggs and tea into their remarkably similarly shaped mouths.

Both waved in salute and gestured to the tea-pot. Bob senior's wife Della, wearing a quilted coat as a dressing gown, asked who wanted eggs and began cooking about a dozen anyway.

'Sleep OK?' Bob junior asked me.

I nodded. It could have been my imagination, but he was talking to me in a completely different way from usual. Normally he smirked at me like a tub full of titters just about to fall over.

This morning he was direct and respectful, like I'd suddenly become a real person. I'll be honest, I hardly recognised the fellow.

While Bob junior asked me solicitous questions and responded to mine in the manner of the young Prince Charles, Bob senior set Charlie up with an inordinate number of vehicles to fix and some wood chopping.

I ate God only knows how many eggs while a West Highland Terrier snuffled at my knees, licking its lips and letting its gummy jaws snap shut. Giving in, I handed it a corner of toast which it noisily devoured while wagging its tail furiously and jumping up on its front paws.

I could see this was a never-ending situation, that no matter how much toast and eggy bits you fed this dog he would never reach satiety. He was condemned, it seemed, to a life of noisy chomping and snuffling and a constant, gnawing desire for foodstuffs.

Charlie suddenly reached out his hand and touched my face. He said he might as well start there and then and Bob junior could drive me home.

I hadn't expected the new year to start quite so abruptly and wondered dismally if that meant I was being driven back to the chalet. Then Charlie gave me his keys and said he'd be home later. Oh well, and at least I had Tess D'Urberville.

From Bob's car I looked out at the bare fields of mid-winter scowling up at the slate-grey sky. Lights sprang on in cold houses where people held their aching heads and tried to make something of this upside-down day.

At Charlie's door I stopped and looked at the house. Shrouded in ivy, it looked like a cottage in a story book except that its whitewash was dirty and the paint round the windows was flaking right down to the original wood.

Maybe Charlie would do that in the spring.

Inside I realised I'd never been here without him. The fact that

65

I was now was every bit as significant as my other visits. I smoked an Embassy Regal I found in a drawer and thought about the first time I had come here and we had gone upstairs to bed. Just like that. How in the world did I ever manage that?

I watched an evening rain shower send waves of water down the kitchen window panes and I could have been looking at the Pacific Ocean on a hot August day, I was so warm and so happy.

13

L ike he said, this house was a new start. He came home that night with cash in his hand and more grease in his hair than a troop of teddy boys, announcing that he was going to paint the living-room tomorrow.

I said I'd help and he said, 'In that case I'll make you breakfast. An egg-free breakfast.'

'Does that mean I'm staying the night?'

'Oh God, yes please, you are staying the night aren't you?' and he sank to his knees and grabbed mine, looking up at me like a saint at the glory of Jesus.

No one had ever wanted me as much as Charlie did. He thought I was a goddess and even when I said things that clanged to the ground under the weight of their naffness, he hung onto my every word.

That night was the first time I got any inkling of this and I was overcome.

When Charlie went upstairs to his bath I sat on the sofa gazing at the blue stems of the gas flames and felt the tears well up in my eyes. They were fat, wet tears that plopped onto my knees like plums.

Charlie shouted down to say he had cigarettes in his jacket if I wanted one and, for a moment, I couldn't speak.

We didn't just paint the living-room, we did all sorts of things together. I kept my job at the café, so we were apart sometimes but I don't really remember that part of it. Except that Lea kept saying how beautiful I looked and she would smile, almost literally, from ear to ear, and her bony cheekbones would stick out like goblins' knees.

She was right. I mean, I looked as beautiful as I possibly could have. My hair shone of its own free will and I must have lost a fair bit of weight because all my clothes suddenly sat on me properly and looked ten times better for it.

Mum watched me come and go and sometimes made complimentary remarks and other times clutched me and uttered warnings about Charlie like some old crone who's just escaped from the attic.

Charlie got a regular stint delivering firewood and I would go with him if I finished in time.

I used to say, 'It's like One Man and his Shadow.'

And Charlie would respond, 'No, it's more like One Man and his Dog.'

Which at least stopped me following him around every day of the week.

Whenever David saw us, he'd make some snidey remark and Charlie would say, 'He's jealous, pure and simple. He suddenly sees you through my eyes and he wants you.'

He added, 'But he's not getting you – is he?'

'Chrissake Charlie.'

The first snow came during the night. We'd just come in from a long drive to houses in need of logs and were hunched over the fire in the room that had recently gone from grey to pink (my choice, and a bad one), when Charlie saw it.

Snow, I don't know, it always gets me. I suppose it does most people. It makes me feel all magical and fairy-taleish and so we went out into the road and watched it twirl onto our hands. It was very dark where Charlie's house was, the last of our meagre streetlights stopped hundreds of yards back. I couldn't see his face properly and even his voice sounded different.

'Are you alright? You sound funny.'

'I'm fine,' he said, but his voice had a crack in it. I didn't understand, I was suddenly confused.

'Charlie?' I hated the dark and not being able to see him and started steering him towards the door. He sniffed and I saw him brush his hand over his eyes in a furtive, impatient gesture.

He sucked in his cheeks with the effort of straightening his face and looked shockingly gaunt.

He didn't say anything when we got in, he just brushed past to the kitchen. I sat down on the edge of the sofa and nervously tapped a cigarette against the packet. When you're so new to each other, some of the firsts you come across can be terrifying. This was his first funny mood and it made me feel like an Alsatian about to be put down by the vet.

He came back to me about ten minutes later, with a bottle of wine and two clean glasses in his hand.

'I'm sorry about that,' he said in a horribly brittle voice.

I looked at him.

'I promise I'll tell you later.'

I nodded.

And he did. We were on our second bottle when he told me about his mother. Who used to like wandering about in the snow.

'She went overboard about everything. If it stopped raining or you got a part in the school play she jumped through hoops. But other times she was almost comatose.'

I just watched him. I had no idea what to say.

'She was a manic depressive. She killed herself when she was thirty-six.'

'Oh Charlie, I'm sorry. I didn't know.' And, 'How old were you?'

'I was in my teens. I was twelve.'

What next, what could I say next?

'What happened, what did she do?' I said, pawing his arm feebly.

'I'm not too sure, I think it was pills. In a way, my dad kept saying, it was a relief because she'd been down for so long by that point he didn't think she would ever come up again. And it was just, it was just . . . unbearable when she was down like that.'

I shifted nearer him and put my arm round his back. He looked at me and smiled and sighed, managing to look soppy and aggressive all at the same time. He took a mouthful of wine and said, in a voice trying hard to be upbeat, 'I just sometimes get a bit upset about it, that's all. It was very sad. But it was a long time ago now. And none of us have happy families.'

And he looked at me and really smiled this time.

'No, I suppose not.' And I smiled back.

When I was brushing my teeth in Charlie's perpetually soggy bathroom I thought about his dad and his being relieved it was all over. And brave enough to say so.

I liked his dad I decided. He probably wore burgundy V-necks and walked around with his hands in his pockets, whistling, and being bravely frank to all who encountered him.

14

The snow fell all that night and by morning it was still pouring out of the sky. The view from Charlie's bedroom was like a scene from Thomas Hardy. The fields rolled out under their thick white blanket and black and red cows lowed mournfully in the distance as they pulled hay from their bales like weary puppies worrying at pillows.

Beyond them, presumably, was the sea but his view of it was as rubbish as ours at home.

We got up to make tea and toast and then ferried it all back into bed. Charlie pulled out a couple of extra blankets from the decrepit wardrobe that kept company with the nearly empty bookshelf and hauled them over us.

'Half an hour,' he said solemnly, putting his freezing cold feet on my thighs. I squealed and nodded and promptly went back to sleep for an hour.

I left him trying to start a car engine that had died of hypothermia and I was late for work but the pipes had frozen and Jimmy hadn't arrived. I pictured him in his van full of rolls, trying to battle through a ten-foot wall of snow but dreaming of the sun on his face.

I hovered, hoping Mary would shut up shop for the day but instead she sent me, with two water canisters, to the water mains tap along by the Drumclair. On my way I realised that Mum would be frozen solid in the chalet and that she wouldn't do anything about it.

71

The previous winter she'd spent days wrapped up in two sleeping bags, smoking solidly while her fingers turned white. School holidays had been the worst because then we'd both be stuck there, me doing wordsearches under the blankets with a torch.

The whole place would smell of gas because we kept the cooker rings on for heat. We must have had rotten headaches but I remember only feeling deadly depressed and that it would never end.

I knew I should do my duty and return home but the thought of going through that again was unbearable.

The same thought must have occurred to Mary because when I got back, she took one look at my face and said, 'Get Ira to come down here. No buts.'

To my surprise she wasn't huddled like a squaw in her robes but shovelling snow off our pitiful little doorstep and listening to the radio.

'You look cold,' I said, and she put her ungloved hands on my cheeks and smiled.

'Mary has some space under her wing and was wondering if you'd like it.'

Nodding at the kettle, she said, 'Cup of coffee first and then Mary.'

When I got inside I saw that she'd packed up her handbag. Its soft black leathery cheeks bulged with cigarette packets and face creams and ointments.

My mother had terrible skin. It flaked away in the cold weather, leaving her cheeks raw and the sides of her mouth cracked. It was already starting again and no amount of ointment seemed able to stop it.

'Were you going somewhere?' I asked when she came in and shut the door.

'I was going to ask her,' she said and my eyebrows must have shot up in surprise. 'I know,' she smiled meekly, 'but I couldn't spend another night like last night. It's too cold. As long as you're OK. Are you OK? Will he take care of you if I'm not at home for a day or two?'

'Of course he will.' And he would, of course. Which made me

72

feel so proud of him. And myself for finding him. I gave my mum a hug, something I never did, and she let out a funny little squeaking noise which meant she was pleased if a little off her guard.

We packed up other things: her pyjamas and socks, sleeping bags, everything from the bathroom.

'Are you on the pill?' she asked.

I nodded. She knew fine well. It was her way of flexing her maternal muscles.

I'd gone on the pill for David, who'd requested it by way of a sweet nothing shortly after we started going out with each other. We didn't actually have sex for months afterwards, and not before everyone knew I was taking regular doses of Microgynon and had achieved the status, therefore, of a minor sex bomb waiting to go off.

The night we first slept together was heralded almost with a fanfare. Bob's elbows must have been badly chaffed with all the nudging he did during the drunken hours leading up to it.

And it was suitably anti-climactic, not that I would admit that to myself at the time. The skin on David's hands was very rough but he made little use of them. Afterwards though, he was very tender and put his arms around me every opportunity he got. He was like a puppy that wanted petting and I loved it but it was the reason I made sure I didn't repeat the exercise with Jocky. Jocky in a state of sexual infatuation, no matter how short-lived, was more than I could stomach.

It was odd but now I couldn't imagine what it must have been like, having sex with anyone other than Charlie. The very idea disgusted me. I could smell Charlie, he seemed to come out of my pores. When we went to sleep at night he leaned into the curve of my spine and his arms cradled mine. If I woke up during the night I would lie there, sensing the texture of his skin against mine and a quiet elation swelling inside me.

As we left, Mum turned off the water and gas and locked up the door. For a second I wondered if we were leaving the chalet for good. That other people would bring in their sleeping bags and plastic cups and plates and have holidays in it.

She gripped my arm all the way down to the road, her tatty little shoes giving way under her at every obstacle.

'Why court shoes?' I asked her impatiently and she shrugged. And, 'What did you do with your figures, you know, your porcelain?'

'I put them away out of sight.'

I had the distinct feeling they were in the carrier bag she was holding like a carry-cot. God, I hoped she didn't fall.

I was just being nosy really, but I came with her to Mary's house, which was upstairs from the café. I'd never been there before but it was just as I'd imagined it. Extraordinarily clean and orderly but overdecorated. The country garden flowers on the walls argued with the imperially striped border; the red and green oilcloth with the farmhouse animals on the crockery; the leaf-flecked curtains with the vines on the sofa.

And everywhere were Lea's dried flowers, sprouting from earthenware pots and vases. But it was as warm as a newly baked cottage loaf and the icy sea looked bright and blue through the picture-book frames of the windows.

Mary took Mum into her guest room, a pristine little cell with white walls and a poppy patterned bedspread. On the wall was a single print of a rosy-cheeked girl paddling at the seashore and by the sink a tiny bar of perfumed pink soap.

Mum let out a sigh and said it was lovely and Mary grunted and said it would just about do. I wondered how soon Mum would whip out the shepherdess and fop ensemble; how soon the sink would be littered with tubes and bottles and the floor with tattered shoes.

I left them to it, smiling shyly at each other like two girls on their first day at boarding school.

Charlie watched me as I unloaded my bags onto the sofa. There wasn't much. A few books, a writing pad, pens, a final batch of knickers and some strawberry scented talc.

'Talc?' he exclaimed, smirking.

'Yeah, talc. All the kids have talc.'

'Oh, uh-huh? And this particular kid is moving in, is she?'

'I can't stay there . . . it's only till the snow stops.'

But I didn't finish that sentence because he was laughing.

'Stay forever. Go on, make an old man happy.'

'Alright,' I shrugged, not at all sure he was being serious or just having a laugh at me because I was eighteen.

'I mean it. I'll paint the bedroom.'

'Only if you choose the colour.'

He made large cow eyes at the pink blush that enveloped us.

'Oh I will, lady.'

Charlie got a lot of work suddenly. The vehicles of the surrounding area had been cursed by some kind of plague and he drove from settlement to settlement, in other people's cars, to lay his healing hands upon them.

He came home so dirty I started buying him Matey bubble bath but the water went black the second he made contact with it and my lovely white bubbles turned into industrial waste.

'Don't leave a black ring,' I'd say as he lay back with a whisky in his hand, closing his eyes and smiling. But he always did.

I cooked terrible meals for us: overcooked spaghetti with mushrooms and tinned tomatoes, or gammon steaks with singed edges. Charlie said I would never make a hausfrau and wondered aloud if he should look around for a replacement. I argued that, having previously had only two gas rings and a toaster at my disposal, my culinary skills were still in their infancy.

It didn't help that, much of the time, I'd had a glass or two of wine beforehand and my perceptions were distinctly muddy.

'I might start eating from bins,' he said once, as he toyed with a fried egg that looked as if it had been dropped from a high building.

'Suit yourself,' I said, spooning mine into an only slightly stale roll.

One night he cooked a paella. He'd finished early and I came home to a warm house filled with an exotic, summer holiday odour.

The scarred skillet was heaped with yellow rice and mussels, red peppers and diced fish, and the sink was a junkyard of knives

75

and bowls. I lit the candle sitting in the middle of the table and read the label on the wine bottle.

'Rioja?'

'You say the J like a K,' he told me.

'Did you learn all this in Spain?' I asked him as I chomped into my most appetising meal for months.

He looked a bit puzzled and said, rather forlornly, 'I've never been to Spain. Anyway, they all eat fish and chips there now.'

'Haven't you?' I was surprised. I suppose it was the Miro poster. I'd assumed he was a Spanish nut, but then, I'd never asked him.

'Nope. I've never been abroad. I don't even have a passport.'

'My God Charlie. That's awful. Why not?'

He shrugged and looked at his fork. 'I don't know. I, Kate, we never got round to it. But you've been?'

Oh yes, I'd been. Every year when Mum and Dad were together we went to desolate resorts around Europe. We wore shorts and sandals and trekked to white churches in the middle of the day and Dad argued with me every time I asked for a Coke. And we'd always go by bus and ferry. Long heaving journeys that I experienced from the toilet, where I threw up my guts. They were my thinnest days.

'Yes. But always with my parents, which meant it was just like being at home except that you couldn't escape to your room.'

'That sounds like fun.'

'Why don't we go?' Suddenly excited. A plan. 'Why don't we go to Spain?'

He looked unenthusiastic and screwed up his eyes. 'You want to?' he asked, like I'd requested he tattoo his face with zodiac symbols.

'You and Kate, you never fancied it?' I meant, what the hell was wrong with you?

He coughed and stated, 'Me and Kate were bored with each other. We were always bored and so we never thought about doing anything.'

'We're not bored, are we?' I asked.

'No.' Very emphatic. 'We could never be bored.'

*   *   *

76

A week later we were standing in the Spar. He had his arm clamped round my shoulder and we were walking around as clumsily as two mismatched children in a three-legged race.

'When are we going to Spain?' he asked.

'Charlie! I thought you didn't want to go.'

'But I do. You were the one going on about being sick in the bogs. I want to watch the sun set over the Alhambra whilst sipping sangria from a terracotta pot.'

'It'll cost.'

'I have, literally, dozens of pounds at my disposal. No, honestly, there's money. So long as you cease with this craze for painting the household.'

'But Charlie . . .'

We ended up in the pub, drinking pints of Guinness while the frozen food thawed and turned its cardboard packaging into mush.

'Some hausfrau you turned out to be,' he said, a fag in his mouth, a pint in each hand, eyeing the soggy mess at my feet.

'I'm more your ornamental,' I said, trying to stifle hiccups.

We were lazy, Charlie and me. We brought out the layabout in each other. We'd paint a wall in a room and it would take us all evening because Charlie would keep stopping to light cigarettes and tell me some daft story, usually against himself, and I would get paint all over my hands and in my hair and become so exasperated with it that I wanted to throw the paint brush out the window.

Sometimes we'd wake to a whole weekend free of work and look out at the fields and talk about driving over to the mainland, or right round the coast. Hours later we'd still be reading bits of the local paper with the breakfast cups strewn around us.

It was maddening really. Once in a while I'd want to run round and round the house, skidding round corners like a cat dispensing its unused hunting adrenaline.

'Come on, let's do something,' I'd almost shout. And Charlie would look at me with a pained expression, reach for a pen, and ostentatiously study the crossword.

15

We'd driven over to Alec's in the afternoon. We only just made it because, as soon as we were in sight of the big black labrador that spent its life nuzzling the frosted glass door, the blizzard began.

It moaned like a cow and blew thick wet snow across the sky. The sea crashed and rumbled in the background but it simply couldn't compete. Charlie parked a few feet from the door and we were caked in ice by the time we barged through it announcing ourselves as we went.

It was just to get money owed by Alec for various things but we stayed for a drink. And then another as the gale caught its breath and reignited itself.

Moira made hamburgers every two or three hours as people began to drift in like fragments of lost tribes. Every time the door banged open, a squall flew in and ran riot through the house, shaking the flames of the fire and tugging at the pages of phone directories before it retreated, exhausted, through the cat flap.

I sat with Moira and her daughter Kayleigh in the kitchen, where it was warm and there was coffee as well as wine. Moira, her grey leisure suit tucked into chunky mountaineering socks which were themselves squeezed into giant tiger-patterned slippers, talked and talked.

She was a fount of scandals, from the women who chucked out a series of men but kept all their furniture to the ferryman who traded stolen car radios and shot himself in the local policeman's bedroom, she knew them all.

Kayleigh sat drawing monsters and men with square bodies and bow ties, perhaps absorbing this sordid refuse for later use as a raconteuse or probably for repeating indiscreetly to her Sunday School teacher.

I wandered through to the living-room from time to time and saw the scene develop from a quiet drink à deux to a rowdy gathering of bawling men clutching Christmas Day measures of Bells. Charlie would look up and smile, patting his bony knee like I was his favourite pup. I'd wave him away and wander back to Moira.

It was a long night, even with the drink. I'd really wanted to get home and have a bath and be alone with Charlie but the weather had conspired to keep us in this house that smelled of dog and Dettol.

Moira, for all her readiness to talk, wasn't very interesting. The stories were a laugh but I actually missed talking to Julia. Not so much because it would be engrossing but because, at the very least, it would be two-way.

I eventually sidled off saying I needed to see how Charlie was getting on and took up his offer, though I sat beside, rather than on him.

That wasn't much better. In here it was Alec who held forth. No wonder the two of them kept to separate rooms. I imagined they just talked over each other continually, the eternally bantering, story-telling couple.

But drink ultimately broke up Alec's domination. Men who had been happy to listen would turn glassy-eyed and launch into breakaway conversations. Usually of the 'Aye, I remember that. And I said to Geordie about it, och, you mind the time . . .' and so on.

I began to feel sick and wandered off to sit in the bathroom awhile, and contemplate Moira's collection of framed animal prints. Stocky Highland cows against a vivid purple sky and sheep nuzzling each other in a soft smirr of rain. To my eyes, they looked a little unhygienic amidst all those guest towels and seahorse-shaped soaps.

When I came down I met Alec on the stairs. He aped a rather tiresome surprised look and then leaned towards me.

'You look gorgeous,' he hissed into my ear, emitting a stream of whisky breath so strong I thought he'd burn my earlobe.

'Hey,' I said in a hearty voice, trying to pass him.

He took my arm, quite roughly though I knew he probably didn't mean it, and stared at me. His eyes were very red and I was so close to his face I could see the thread veins across his cheeks, some of them so pronounced they were almost purple.

'Talk to me,' he cajoled, and my heart sank.

I've always hated the boring drunk man in need of a talk. The old geezers in pubs who stagger up to you, an oily glint in their eye, and pronounce that it is your lucky day. Not your lucky day because they have a ten thousand pound cheque in their pocket for you or anything, but because they are going to buy you a drink and make you pay for it by boring a hole in you till closing time.

'I need to tell you about Charlie,' he said, slumping down onto one of the stairs and half-pulling me down with him.

I sat obediently, hoping someone's bladder would soon reach capacity and compel them to come up the stairs. But I couldn't be rude and walk away.

'D'you know,' he said in a half-stifled belch, 'D'you know why Kate went away?'

I shook my head. I couldn't be bothered with this.

'She went away,' he began ponderously, trying to line up his glass with his mouth and failing several times, 'Because . . . he, that bugger down there, he couldn't keep himself sober for an hour at a time.' Another attempt at the glass. 'He's drunk, he's a drunk. And he won't change.'

It was almost funny, being told Charlie was a drunk by a man who was barely sober enough to sit upright on his own stairs, but it was actually too boring to be funny.

'He's not, he's fine,' I said shortly, trying to say, 'That's me, I'm away now' with my eyes.

Alec waved his hands. Oh God, he was far from finished. 'Ah! he's fine now. I'll give him that. He's very good, I'll give him that. But he has to be (hic) to impress you.'

I made a sound of protest and he raised his hand imperially.

'No, you just don't know. Kate would find him lying on the floor, the floor (he gestured down the stairs with a heavy sweep of his arm and almost toppled down them) most nights. She couldn't stand it.'

He lurched again and I caught his arm. Then I looked down the stairs and saw Charlie standing there, completely still. I couldn't tell if he was looking at me or Alec but I could see that this erstwhile private conversation had suddenly become a problem.

Alec continued, oblivious, 'We had to help her . . . you know . . . get going . . . Ah, I don't know, I'm a bit pissed . . .'

I ignored him, stood up and went down to Charlie, catching his arm as I passed. He jerked his elbow to throw off my hand and stood a minute, glaring up at Alec who simply shrugged and stared at his glass.

Alec seemed to be impervious behind his glassy wall of alcohol. I'm not sure he was aware of Charlie, or even that I wasn't sitting beside him any more.

But Charlie was intensely aware of him.

He said something, I didn't catch it, as I led us back into the living-room where the queasy party atmosphere curdled at the sight of Charlie and his white face.

Alec appeared a minute later and stood quietly at the door. He and Charlie stared at each other and I suddenly realised that they were both poisonously drunk and about to lunge at each other.

I was monstrously embarrassed, mostly because I couldn't get Charlie to even so much as look at me, but I was also very angry. Like most people, I'm deeply unnerved by violence and the feeling manifests itself, perhaps unfortunately, as a boiling desire to kill everybody involved. I pulled at Charlie's arm as aggressively as I could and he stumbled without turning.

A split second later he looked at me and I got a brief flash of the face that met mine when he blasted me at his front door. Then it faded.

'It's alright,' he said, 'I should go.'

'You can't do that,' said Moira, who seemed to be the only

81

person capable of steering this situation. 'But this man' – and here she jerked her thumb at her husband like she was hitching a lift – 'can leave for his bed. He's had enough to sink a battleship.'

Her voice was very high and imperious and Alec eyed her viciously. But then, extraordinarily, he put his glass down on the sideboard and allowed himself to be led away. The room breathed a sigh of relief.

'Charlie, what the hell?' asked Gary, a huge man of forty with cheeks like corned beef.

Charlie shrugged, accepted a glass of whisky, settled down in a chair and was silent.

I don't remember going to bed, only suddenly being there, with Charlie spread out beside me, snoring with his mouth open. He looked foul and he reeked of drink. There was an empty bottle by the bed and I hoped to God that hadn't been us. Or, even worse, just him. I tried to get back to sleep but my hangover wouldn't let me. Lying there, with dirty streaks of light filing through the gaps under the curtains, I felt alone for the first time in what seemed like months.

Hours later I tried to rouse him and he groaned and rolled over. He felt like someone I didn't know.

I was terribly thirsty, so much so it was all I could think about, but the sound of footsteps in the house around me made me stay where I was. Meeting Alec was the last thing I needed.

We left late afternoon. The house was empty but we were too stunned with hangovers to talk to each other. I shouldn't have let him drive the car because he was still drunk but I wanted to leave too much to stop him.

He drove with an almost demented concentration and I tried to concentrate too.

When we got home we went back to bed. We didn't even switch on the lights.

16

Kate and Charlie, Charlie and Kate. From being someone I barely considered, a shred of curtain adhering to a rail, Kate suddenly walked on centre-stage – holding Charlie by the hand.

I thought they were bored. Bored was good for me. Anything other than bored and their marriage took on alarming dimensions. It overhung the present like a high curved cliff, making me small and barely visible.

Yesterday I had been his sunshine. Today I made up the numbers in the shade. Certainly that's how it felt as I trudged through those long few days that followed the blizzard. The house was murderously cold and I felt more sick and headachey than I had thought it possible to feel.

Mum, who came into the café surprisingly few times considering she lived upstairs from it, said I looked like shit.

'You look like shit,' she would say, sounding like one of those annoyingly hip grannies you get on 'real' people TV shows.

Not that she was wrong in her observations. Any improvement my appearance had taken on since Christmas had been well and truly wiped away. I looked like I'd spent the last ten months in a basement, eating biscuits.

Charlie was morose. He talked to me, of course, and we ate together but we were like two people making conversation because we were sharing a train journey.

We both still managed to go to work. I gathered that he and Alec were speaking to each other and that this mood that bunched around us was not specifically related to Alec's social shortcomings.

When we were together in the house we drifted around each other. I painted bits and pieces or washed things, filled in shopping surveys, there was always something. Charlie did likewise. We lay in bed together without touching.

I read grimly, trying to concentrate on the downfall of Tess D'Urberville but finding that, after half an hour, I could still be labouring through the same descriptive passage without the faintest idea of where I was.

I thought about Kate for hours at a time. I thought about her in the café, on the walk home, when I tried to fall asleep. Her hair changed every time, finally settling on shoulder length and blonde.

'She looked like an art teacher. She wore big boots and lots of dark colours,' Lea told me. Kate strode through green and russet fields with her hair billowing out behind her like the ribbons from a maypole. Her jersey was bottle green and her lips a Paris red.

I wondered why he bothered coming home, it had become so like a tired old marriage. But, I had to remind myself, this was his home. The real question was, what was I doing in it?

I was a squalid brown shape whose nose ran when it cried.

It was of some consolation that I didn't have the option of moving out just yet. If the weather had been mild and the chalet a little more habitable, then I would have had to make up my mind. The snow ensured that I didn't have to.

We drank a huge amount, but in an anti-celebratory way. For the first time I could drink the best part of a bottle of wine and actually feel more sober and sad than I'd felt to begin with. Charlie, on the other hand, become brutally cheerful, uttering perfectly upbeat responses to my monotonous 'do you want me to hang around or whats' without, it seemed, communicating at all. His eyes slid from my gaze every time.

He had lost all interest in me and, with enough alcohol inside him, he could be calm and frank about it. It wasn't going to work, he'd been a fool to think so. I was a harmless little person but Kate, she was the one. Any mention of her and he tumbled headfirst into the hole she'd left him in.

Now he was just waiting for the bad weather to end and for me, in the natural course of things, to go with it.

The possibility that he might have a serious drink problem did also occur to me. But it didn't concern me, not in the least. Maybe she did find him lying on the floor. Maybe it was only once, maybe she made it up, maybe it happened every day of the week and twice on Sundays. It didn't concern me – she did. She was a phantom fatale who had strode on in and ruined everything.

Julia came in to see me one day. Unlike my mother, she refrained from delivering a beauty critique.

'I've some gossip for you,' she said, as I carried two teas to the table. I sat down and drank most of mine in one gulp.

'Lorraine's pregnant.'

I was going to say that was hell of a quick but remembered that, in fact, she and David had been a couple for about six months. I just thought they were a new thing because I'd never taken them seriously. I'd assumed their relationship was as skin-deep as ours had been.

Maybe it was. It didn't take feelings or commitment to get someone up the stick.

Instead I said something like 'Oh' and noted how little I cared. The only thing in the world that interested me was what Charlie thought about when he thought about Kate. Lorraine could cook and eat her own hair for all I cared.

Julia continued and I could see that she was excited.

'I think her and David might get married.'

I couldn't think why that would excite her.

'Are you going to be a bridesmaid?'

'No, don't be silly.'

And then, with a big clanking noise inside my brain, the penny dropped. She hoped the wedding of his best mate would make Bob want to marry. I didn't bother mentioning that nothing puts a man off matrimony like the sight of his best mucker in a morning suit.

'What's Bob saying to it?' I wondered, without a splinter of interest.

'He's . . . I don't know. Not much.'

How could she want that, I wondered. Being the new Della, making breakfast for forty and never being spoken to.

'*You're* not pregnant, are you?' I asked, all of a sudden.

'No!' she shouted, looking outraged and also a little bit guilty. The idea had occurred to her then.

'No,' she said again, meeting my eyes.

She tried to persuade me to come out for a drink with her but I didn't have the heart for it. All I would do was pine to be home with Charlie and, when I got there, break my heart over the fact that he had failed to notice.

This whole time was just over a week but in my memory it has stretched into a block as big as a school term. It's very big and I find it hard to believe it was that bad. But I can't remember there being any let-ups, my mind just used the same crayon to colour in all of it.

I was lying on the bed. Lying on the bed and looking at the wall in front of my face. I felt him come into the room and I didn't bother, for once, turning round.

When he sat down beside me I nearly jumped out of my skin. He didn't look upbeat any more. Instead, his face seemed to have sunk inwards and I don't think I'd ever seen anyone look so tragic.

'You're not going to stay, are you?' he said, in a voice that emanated from the bottom of the ocean.

'I don't think you want me to anymore.'

'I do, but I don't think you want to.'

This was irritating already. I hated it when people deflected things onto me because they couldn't spit out what they meant. Oh, you're too good for me, you don't want me etcetera ad nauseam. Why couldn't they just say things?

'What's happened, Charlie?'

'I've been a prick. I've been the way I was with Kate and that's why she left.'

86

Oh God, not her again.

He saved our relationship by continuing, 'The difference is that I wanted her to leave. We were two people who should never have been married. But I don't want you to leave, I really don't.'

He finished in a rush and looked as if he was about to be sick.

I sat up properly and put my arms round him and buried my head on his chest.

'It won't ever happen again, I promise,' he said and I nodded.

I lifted my head and kissed him and his return kiss was urgently sexual. A thrill ripped through me like a hot wire.

Afterwards he lit us both a cigarette, something he hadn't done in ages.

'Forgive me?' he said.

I nodded happily. I had no idea what I was forgiving him for.

17

In February something strange occurred. My father arrived. I hadn't seen him since I was eight years old and at first he seemed to have aged terribly but, as the days passed, my perception adjusted and he became just as I remembered him.

Mum and me went back to the chalet two weeks after the blizzard and we both felt almost guilty at the sight of it. Like Mole, we'd left because something more interesting had come along and it had taken the abandonment badly.

The big picture window in the living-room had let in water and the upholstery on the window seat was sodden. You pressed your fingers into it and a tiny pool of water formed round them. The formica of the table had warped and the bare ends, where the woodchip showed through, were soaked.

My bedroom was so cold I couldn't tell if it was wet or not. Mum looked unbelievably tired at the sight of it all.

'How are you and Charlie? Can you stay on at his?' she asked.

I nodded. I was going to do that anyway.

'I'm going to leave it until the weather improves. I'll get someone to fix that window and maybe I could take these cushions and dry them out at Mary's.'

I nodded. It was like visiting a sick relative who smelled bad. I just wanted to get away.

On our journey to Mary's, soggy sofa cushions under each arm, she warned me that Dad had been in touch.

'He phoned the Drumclair, can you believe that? When was I last to be found in pubs?'

She didn't phone him back, even though he had phoned several times and left his number on each occasion. Apparently the staff were furious about it because he was so surly. He might still turn up, she supposed, and doubtless someone would direct him to us.

If this had happened six months before, even two months before, I'd have been jumping up and down in excitement. Not so much because I wanted to see him but because he might take me away with him to London. Now I just thought, what a bloody nuisance.

We were eating tinned spaghetti and sausages in front of the gas fire while two of the window seat cushions belched out acrid steam on either side of us.

'Don't you want to see him?' asked Charlie.

'I don't know. I suppose I'm curious, but that's all. What about your Dad, you got on well with him, didn't you?'

Charlie snorted and said with a nastiness that was struggling to sound ironic, 'What the hell gave you that idea? We hated each other.'

'I didn't know that, sorry. I thought . . .' Why was it I thought that again? 'I thought you did.'

'Doesn't matter,' he smiled, 'But yours, you got on OK, didn't you?'

I suppose we did. Mum and Dad used to fight all the time. I remember my mum always being at the top of the stairs, shouting down at him that he could go to hell. I would sidle around the corners of the house and find a place to sit Sindy down and do her hair. I remember once my dad standing over me, looking down and saying rather unkindly, 'So you're going to be a hairdresser? That's really something.'

Shortly after that I went through a phase, like a week or something, where I had to keep washing my hands. I'd be outside playing with my friends and my hands would get slippery with sweat and if I came in contact with the ball and then someone else touched it, I would have a panic attack. I thought I was passing on disease and I had to run indoors and wash my hands. I thought I was going to kill them with my germs and I couldn't think of anything else for thinking of that.

But it passed. One day it must have just gone.

'What happened when he left?' Charlie asked. By now we were on our way to the Drumclair, to get out of the house that smelled like a dank mattress.

'I'm not too sure. He came into my room really late and kissed me on the head and said goodnight. And in the morning Mum was shouting to herself in the kitchen.'

I ran downstairs because I thought there was someone there that she was shouting at, and she turned to me and yelled, 'We'll have to sell the house because of your bloody father.'

I stepped backwards, retracing my steps like dogs do when they're being shouted at.

Dad used to take me to the petrol station when he was filling up the car and then we'd drive around the housing estate where we lived, looking at the new builds and wondering how many rooms they would have.

The smell of petrol and builders' sand makes me think of my father driving his car on sunny Saturday mornings.

'Why here, though? Why did she move the two of you here?' asked Charlie, putting a pint of 80/- in front of me and pulling cigarettes out a new packet so tightly packed, several came at once.

'We came here once on holiday and it didn't cost much. Mum couldn't get a mortgage. The neighbour,' I said, realising I'd never said this out loud before, 'I think she had an affair with my Dad. I think that's why he left in the end, because Mum found out and gave him such a hard time about it.'

'I don't blame her, fucking hell.'

'No, I don't either. It was him, he couldn't handle being in the wrong. I think, I mean, I'm only guessing. She never told me and I didn't ask.'

'Any reason why not?'

I shrugged, 'Who knows? We just don't talk like that. Mum

90

doesn't know how to open up to people and I learned that from her. I mean, I can talk to you but I can't to her. It would be like watching her have sex.'

Charlie said Dad could stay with us if I wanted him to.

'I like the 'us',' I said.

'Well, it is us now, isn't it?'

But he didn't come and didn't come and I began to forget that he ever would. Until one night, very late, there was an almighty bang on the door. We were in bed, not sleeping, but it was late and very dark.

If it wasn't about a road accident, there was only one person it could be.

Charlie opened the door and Dad stood there, leaning on the door frame looking as angry as he had that time he called me a hairdresser.

'I'm looking for . . .' and then he saw me. 'Karen?' His face turned up in a soppy smile and, pushing past Charlie he came towards me and took my chin in his hand and then all of me in his arms.

For a second I was frozen and then I clutched him, feeling an absurd choke of tears in my throat.

From far away I could hear Charlie shut the door and I could almost hear him smile too.

We sat in the kitchen, all of us shivering with the cold, and drank brandy and coffee. We'd run out of cigarettes but Dad seemed to have about twenty packets stored around his person. His very black hair was slicked back and he wore a white shirt and vest under his navy blue V-neck sweater.

He looked like what he was, a ducker and diver, a small-time dealer and nearly conman trying to ape the respectability of a schoolteacher. The effect of his tidy sweater and cords was ruined by the gold signet ring on his pinkie and his gaff lad hairstyle.

'Whose house is this then?' he asked, looking round the room like he was thinking of thieving it.

'Mine,' said Charlie, 'and hers.'

'I've got a nice little place down in London. Not as good as the old place, but getting there,' said Dad.

91

He didn't say much really. He was settled, apparently, made quite good money and knew a lot of good people.

I told him desultory details of my life, trying to sound wry, like it was all rather amusing.

'You're not doing very well, are you?' he asked. He couldn't help it. If he saw a face he just had to slap it. I shrugged and looked at Charlie, who winked and asked him if he had a fridge freezer.

I kept looking at Dad and trying to remember what the wife next door had looked like. She had thick black hair that she wore in plaits. They flanked her face like two lengths of rope and she wore denims that hugged her hips and showed off her belly, which was very white and round, like a bar of fancy soap.

'Have you seen Mum yet?' I asked. The brandy had filled me with an emotionalism that felt as cloying as a wet tracksuit I didn't have the energy to take off.

He shook his head, 'I don't think that would be a very good idea, do you?'

Charlie called it to a halt right there by saying we needed to go to bed, we had work in the morning. It was already four a.m., but Dad nodded and allowed himself to be led to the empty room upstairs where Jocky used to sleep. It was so cold you could see your breath, but Dad didn't seem to notice.

Already, I felt unbelievably glum about him being around, like someone had put an anvil on a chain round my neck. The man who drove his car and liked to look at new houses actually lived in my imagination. The real one was this shabby creature who competed with you and tried to make you feel bad.

Charlie hugged me and said nothing. I wished I'd been brought up by gypsies who'd spurned me at the age of sixteen, and I think he wished I had too.

18

He stayed for nearly a week. By the end of that time he and my mother were at least being civil to one another and they even managed to have a drink together without one of them storming off with some juicy lingo emanating from their mouth.

But he just made me angrier and angrier. He stayed with us every night, ate with us, went to the pub with us, and we'd just be getting into some kind of conversation when he'd pitch in with some crap remark about me, and how I didn't seem to 'be amounting to very much'. Charlie always waded in with something that either shut the old bastard up or concluded the evening.

The next day Dad would always be apologetic and say it was only his way of showing concern. But he'd get back on the subject soon enough.

The problem was that, no matter what I said in my defence, he'd sigh and shake his head with an infuriating little smile. I told him that I was thinking of sitting some Highers and maybe using them to get into college and I might as well have said I was saving up for a boob job before trying my luck in Hollywood.

'You're just not being practical,' he'd say, wagging his head.

'So what is fucking practical?' I demanded once, zipping up my jacket so fiercely I hit myself under the chin with my hand.

That stumped him. For a nanosecond. He suggested I get myself 'something by way of a trade'.

A couple of times I thought Charlie was going to take him outside and stove in his head with a shovel. Instead he would settle for a patient reiteration of my qualities. I was amazed he thought I had so many. Apparently I was one of the smartest women he'd ever met and, if anyone around here was going to do anything with their lives, it would be me.

I raised my eyebrows at that and he nodded.

'I mean it. You will.'

Dad shook his head like someone had cracked a corny joke and, again, I had that shovel-and-cranium presentiment.

Finally he left and I felt like fumigating the house to get rid of the bad vibes.

'We should have asked him to leave,' I said to Charlie.

'You only had to give the nod,' he replied.

Dammit. Why hadn't I?

Mum called round at the house the day after he'd gone. I was very surprised because she had never approached Charlie's house before. She was carrying a bouquet made up of three different colours of carnations wrapped up in crinkly cellophane and numerous elastic bands.

'I'm sorry honey,' she said, looking smaller than ever. I seemed to tower over her like a big furry bear.

'Why? You didn't invent him.'

'I know, but I should have told him to leave you alone and stay at the hotel. Well, I did actually, but I should have insisted.'

My mum insisting was a bit like a hamster taking pops at a tiger, but never mind, I suppose she did her best.

I made her coffee in the kitchen and she stood on ceremony, her hands holding her handbag to her stomach, and gave nervous little smiles at me as she nodded at things she liked, such as the kettle and the salt and pepper mills. She gave an especially vehement non-verbal tweak to display her liking for the blue and yellow spotted ashtray, made I think by Charlie as a schoolboy. Or certainly someone of school age with the uncertain idea that cigarettes were the size of tablespoons.

'You don't need to tell me what he was like,' she began all of a sudden, 'I know very well what he was like. He's actually quite a nice man, deep down, and I know you know that too.'

I nodded hesitantly, thinking petrol stations.

94

She sat down, sort of sideways, as if she were incapable of bending in the middle. Had she been a member of the contemporary dance world she'd have been a wow, so instinctively did she utilise physical language to express her emotions. She felt awkward and so she moved like an elderly robotic dancer trying to manoeuvre his way onto a bucket seat.

With schoolmarmish precision she continued, 'I had it all planned, what I was going to say, but I said it all much better in the car . . .'

'You drove from the café?' I interrupted, clinging to this vestige of banality lest we drown in, God forbid, something as overwhelming as a real conversation.

She smiled a pinched little smile and looked disappointed. Leaving me with no option but to take the plunge.

'And what . . . eh . . . did you say in the car?'

'Oh, it doesn't matter.' Pause. Then a huge intake of breath, like she was gearing up for the chorus of 'The Holly and the Ivy', and, 'I've thought about it so many times and I've realised a few things. I realised when I saw him again just how angry he made me.' A pause as she broke surface for air. 'How he always had to be cleverer than everyone else and right all the time, how he always had to criticise people all the time and bring everything down. And I think what I'm trying to say . . .'

She stopped, bewildered as a (panting) dog in traffic.

'. . . is that.'

Every vein in her body appeared to be protruding like tree roots and her face was very red.

'Sorry,' she said, giving a little giggle that was so high pitched it sounded like a budgie.

She took another deep gulp, this time of coffee, and added, 'That's why he never had any friends.'

'Oh,' I said stupidly, 'he had one. That Mrs Thing from next door, the one, you know the one, with the pla . . .' At which point I stopped and made one of those 'Me and My Big Mouth' gestures and gaped at the floor.

She looked at me with surprising calmness and said, 'I didn't think you knew about her.'

'I didn't. I was just guessing.'

'Well, it was a good guess, and correct.'

Calm. Then another inhalation of the four winds to fuel the atomic bomb-sized follow-up, the force of which actually propelled her to her feet.

'He couldn't let that be his fault either, it had to be mine. And it can't be his fault that we live in a run-down bloody fucking holiday home. That has to be mine too.'

She then took out an extraordinarily long cigarette with a white filter and shakily lit it with a Victoria Wine lighter. For my part, I was so stunned that she was saying real things to me, as opposed to bonkers suggestions that I train to be a lollipop lady, that I didn't know what to say. So I said the first thing that came into my head.

'Have you told Mary?' What? Why?

At which she regained the power to bend, and sat down. 'This is a family matter,' she said, quite censoriously but quite gently too.

'What family's that then?' I asked jovially enough but our eyes met and I realised we understood each other as completely as a good key fits into its lock.

Clunk, scratch, click. Got it. I remember talking to someone for the first time, this is years later, telling him this long convoluted story about a film I'd seen where two drunks try to raise the devil and, on the appointed night, the door of their apartment swings open and a black goat walks in. It made your hair stand on end but it was completely ambiguous, I said, but he was nodding already, saying, 'That's good. I get it.' And Mum and me, you see, we got it, and it was remarkable.

'Some families are better for having the air about them,' she softly shrugged. 'Yes, I see that now. It took me a while.'

As I watched her leave, about an hour later, I felt rather bleak. Eight years it had taken her to figure that out and another ten years or so before to get to the point of needing to start figuring it out. It had come too late, I thought. I mustn't let that happen to me.

*   *   *

96

Charlie couldn't get over him. He kept doing Dad impressions, pulling back his hair from his forehead and shaking his head sorrowfully as I was halfway through an amusing anecdote about café society.

Dad's visit seemed to affect him for longer than it did me. I was just relieved he'd gone but Charlie continued to be obsessed, bringing him up over and over again like a bad meal I'd prefer to forget.

'Drop it, Charlie. Entertain me instead with your wit and repartee.'

'Alright then, here's one you'll like, missus. What do you call a greasy haired mini-cab driver with the dress sense of Ken Barlow? Yes, your old dad.'

Funnily enough, not long after, I received a letter from Dad with a cheque for four hundred quid in it. 'Do something interesting,' he advised. So I did. I booked a holiday in Spain for two.

19

As soon as I signed up for it I sensed that I was in trouble. I didn't know why but I knew that Charlie would be annoyed with me. Not in the macho-man, let-me-pay-I've-got-a-penis kind of way that, say, David would have been capable of. More a kind of disappointed fatherly kind of annoyed. Much the same way as my father, had he known, would have reacted.

Unlike those wily women you read about who keep new Max Mara suits out of sight for years, I blurted it all out to Charlie a mere half hour after I'd blown what I assumed was my entire inheritance on a fortnight in Ibiza.

He'd come to pick me up from work in a rather spanking red Volvo belonging to a retired headmaster who believed Charlie when he said it would take at least two weeks to fix.

'We're going to Spain,' I announced, in the voice of a small boy who's just emptied the teapot over the baby and has decided he might as well admit it and get it over with.

Charlie smiled and said, 'I know.'

'No, I mean we're really going. I mean, we've got tickets and everything.'

'Oh, I see,' he responded, looking at the gearstick.

We drove the hundred yards home in silence. Charlie appeared to be thinking.

He brought it up later. He wasn't angry or authoritative, just very determined about reimbursing me for the entire amount.

'How much?' he kept demanding in a voice that, like the sea, would eventually erode a thousand feet of cliff-face.

I didn't have a big thing about money. Which was just as well really because I very rarely had any. But I didn't dwell on having or not having it. In my experience it was always men who got worked up about the girth of their wallet while women accepted their cashflow situation like they did the weather – it came, it went, you moaned anyway.

I'd as soon have spent the £400 as not but I gave in because Charlie wanted me to. I named the price of two weeks in Santa Eulalia and he told me I would have it back the next day.

'But . . . ?'

'I'm old enough to be your father. At least let me behave like I am.'

'But he never paid for anything in his life.' Actually that wasn't true but the moment screamed out for it.

'And I hope there's a lot of other things he didn't do,' said Charlie as I slithered clumsily onto his knee.

'Maybe I could buy some new clothes then,' I said, realising that almost everything I was wearing belonged to him. And, I reflected sadly, not looking that much more feminine for my being inside them.

'I like you in my things,' he said, I don't know how much from gallantry, before adding, 'But I am running out.'

So that was it. Spain was booked and I still had enough money for ten pairs of Levis and a round at the local.

After that, maybe even because of that, my living with Charlie became official. I realised this had happened because, one afternoon, Charlie came home and told me that he'd met Julia and she'd asked if his house was the place to find me.

'I said it was, that you lived here now,' he said, adding, with his hands held up in a canine begging posture and his head on one side, 'Did I do right?'

'Yeah,' I smiled. But my smile quickly faded. 'Do you think Julia will think she and the gang can just come round here now?'

'Don't you want them to?'

'It's just that . . .' just that I liked things the way they were, just him and me, but even I knew that sounded clingy and needy and unattractive.

'It's just that they're all awful,' I said instead.

Charlie thought this was hilarious.

'Well, yes, they are,' he agreed, 'But so are my friends. People are, by their very nature, bloody awful. But there's good sides to them too. Julia, for a start, really cares about you.'

I eyed him suspiciously, wondering if her dwarf-like flirting had finally got to him but he looked serious.

'Maybe,' I said, unconvinced. Then again, she had been the one who understood – even before I did – about Charlie.

'Anyway, I think she wants to see you about something.'

'It'll be about David and Lorraine getting married probably,' I said, opening the kitchen cupboard to survey our bountiful haul of withered vegetable matter.

'Are they?' he asked, startled.

I tended to forget, to be honest, that Charlie had any connection with David and his family. He didn't really, I suppose. His brother, who hadn't ever come near us for no reason in particular as far as I could see, had married into the clan, and that was all. Charlie's only duty had been to help out on the accommodation front once – and we all know how that went.

No wonder they weren't issuing invitations to family pow-wows. But I was concerned that Charlie might be hurt by this.

'It's only a rumour told to me by Julia. Actually, no, made up by Julia,' I said, plopping a series of wizened carrots into the bin and wondering if it was true, that advert where they put hand-cream on a dried up leaf and it springs back into youthful suppleness.

'I didn't expect to be the first to know, Karen, don't worry about that.'

'Are they pissed off about, you know, that night with Jocky?'

And here he smirked, rather a lovable smirk if you can imagine such a thing. 'Not as much as you'd think. Your mum, for instance, would have garrotted me probably. Louise was fucked off, and she's stayed that way but she never liked me anyway, so it was a good excuse to hang it on.'

'Oh, why?'

'Friend of Kate's.'

'Oh.' I moved onto potatoes and found them to be the source of the slightly putrid smell that had haunted the kitchen for a week or so now.

'So you're surprised about David?' I asked.

'Yes, a bit. I take it he's got her into trouble, as my old granny would say?'

'Yes. He's making a mistake, isn't he?'

'On the contrary, I think it's a splendid idea. If he's going to make a housewife out of . . . whatsit? Lorraine? that means he can't make one out of you.'

Julia did come round to the house, but she checked with me at the café first.

'He won't mind?' she asked, like I lived with Bluebeard and I was really keen on going into that bloody chamber at the end of the hall.

'He'll make rock-buns, he'll be so pleased,' I reassured her.

I was very touched, even though it made the beginning of the evening as awkward as a sixth year school disco. Julia arrived arm in arm with Bob, who was carrying a bunch of extravagant blooms – Marks and Spencer, I could tell – and beaming sweatily.

Julia had brought a box of wine which she suggested she and I drink at home while 'the boys' went out. I looked at Charlie, who had put on his what-a-fantastic-idea face, even though I knew that sitting in a boozer with Bob was his idea of hell. He smiled at me, and at Bob and Julia, and put on his jacket.

Julia took the flowers into the kitchen and Bob followed her and looked around uncertainly. The absence of matey banter made him uneasy but I knew Charlie, he wouldn't let him suffer for long.

'Wrap up warm now,' I whispered into Charlie's face, wrapping his scarf round and round his neck until it nearly obscured his mouth.

'I love you,' he said, then hastily kissed me on the lips and made for the door.

I stared after him but he only turned to look back after he'd put his arm round Bob and steered him into the early evening dusk. Looking over Bob's head, he caught my eye for a second, and was gone.

I was on such a high I could have listened to Julia talk about crochet and what dreams she'd been having lately. As it happened, I didn't have to because she had a whole trough of fascinatingly trivial dung to impart to me and, unlike Moira, she wanted to hear my take on it too.

She was also an expert with boxes of wine. Had it been me we'd still have been awaiting our first drink when the boys got home. But Julia, she could navigate the most frustrating of mechanisms without a hitch. Just shows what endless rounds of girls' nights in can do for one. I, personally, preferred ring-pulls.

She looked odd in our kitchen and I wasn't a hundred per cent sure I liked her being there. I suppose it was because things with me and Charlie had been so intense and I hated the thought of anything diluting it and other people getting in our way. I didn't feel secure enough to trust us to the world.

'Now, I've got a confession,' began Julia, bringing two giant measures of white wine to the table, 'and that is that I've actually become quite friendly with Lorraine Parker. Oh God, Karen, please say you don't mind.'

When she was stressed out about something, Julia always talked very fast. The last part of that sounded more like 'ohgo-karnpleasay'donemine' but I knew what she meant because it was what she used to say after eating all my crisps or telling Suzanna I'd been sick in my hood. She'd always be stricken with remorse, as she was now, and I was always gracious, because I had no choice.

This time, for once, I was gracious out of choice. That, and not having the faintest who Lorraine Parker was.

Then it dawned, and I laughed.

'Really? Her? Is she OK then?'

Julia closed her eyes and took a gulp of wine and nodded.

'Yeah, she's alright. She can be a bit mumsy and a bit know-all but yeah, she's OK. Knows how to handle David, that's for sure. Oh God, Karen . . . sorry, that sounds all wrong.'

An hour later, and with most of the Oh God, Karens out the way, we were heavily into You remember him, him with the ulcer scar territory.

Various people I knew had become, or stopped being, alcoholics, one had died and one had nearly moved away but not gone through with it. Meantime David, it seemed, had agreed to become a blushing bridegroom and Lorraine and he were even looking at houses.

Julia's mother, the one who insisted on being a sister rather than a parent, said it would be Bob next. I looked at Julia and she guffawed.

'Can you imagine?' she said, 'I'm as likely to get Bob Geldof down the aisle. Wait, oh God, even he's married. Is he? I can't remember.'

'Does it matter?' I asked.

'I don't know,' she said, twisting her glass round and round in her hands, 'I don't know, honestly. I wonder if I really love him or if it's just what's expected of me.'

'I bet your mum likes him.'

'Oh aye,' she said, so emphatically that I nearly spat out all my wine with laughing.

By the time the boys came home we were so full of wine and the spirit of talk that we were practically bawling at each other.

'Ladies, ladies,' said Charlie in mock horror.

All the clasps had fallen, one by one, from Julia's wiry, curly hair. Browny blonde corkscrews bounced above her forehead and around her shoulders. It looked a little better than her usual, prim, pinned-in style. She fluffed it demonstratively in the tiny hall mirror on the way to the toilet and said, 'At last, beauty.' Or something like that.

She didn't return from the bathroom for ages and eventually I had to go up and knock on the door loudly enough to wake her because, as she often did, she'd settled for a spot of shuteye while about her sitting-down toilette.

Bob had stayed remarkably sober. This was something Bob did, which meant that he could drive everyone home and recount precisely what kind of a show you'd made of yourself in front of all your friends.

I'd once said to Charlie that I didn't know how Julia could stand going out with someone who hardly touched a drink. He didn't say anything at all in response which is why I remember it, because Charlie very rarely said nothing to me.

Bob helped the now limp Julia out the front door and smiled at her with – or did I imagine it? – affection. I didn't see them drive away because, apparently, I had fallen fast asleep at the bottom of the stairs.

20

The winter began to pass. Suddenly you weren't walking home in the dark any more and you didn't need to race to the toilet and back during the night because of tomb-like temperatures in the corridor.

We had worked hard and now our selection of bare brown and grey walls had metamorphosed into acres of green, yellow and blue. Charlie even repainted the living-room's unfortunate pink with a more palatable lilac while I spent an entire week on my knees in the bedroom painting the skirting boards.

Eventually everybody came to call and would find us paint-daubed and frantic, like a couple of 1960s pop artists with a giant gallery show in a week and not a canvas ready. And they always brought something, not just flowers but also breadknives and tablecloths and – I'm not sure who – a set of toothbrushes for an electric toothbrush. Somewhat grubby if I remember rightly.

Mum never asked what my plans were. She just came into the café one day and told me the chalet now belonged to someone else. She fawned over me for about half an hour, sorrowfully repeating that we were now without a 'family home', but I quickly cottoned on to the fact that she was as delighted to slam the door on that damp shoebox of a residence as I was. I had no problems saying adieu to a home so small you kept getting slapped in the face by your washing and so dank it got you worrying about trenchfoot.

'So you're going to live with Mary?' I asked.

She clutched my arm and gave a mock giggle that made me think of drag queens, saying, 'Don't say it like that – people will think we're funny.'

I needn't tell you what she meant by that, only that it took me hours to work it out. Funny? Mary and her couldn't be funny if Tony Hancock wrote the scripts.

I was happy with Charlie. We seemed to have settled into a life with each other that fitted like a pair of old shoes but ones I'd fight to the death over. I felt that, if I hadn't been here all my life then it was because I'd been on my way. Everything that had ever happened to me had been a stepping stone to this.

I loved him, and I'd never felt anything even remotely like it. I'd very much wanted to love people and I'd assumed that, because I thought I could fancy the idea of marrying him, I loved David. Like hell I did. I just had to look at Charlie or hear his voice and my heart seemed to turn over.

He made me feel that I was a good person, that I was worth something.

It didn't matter that, after midday, I rarely saw him without a drink. Everyone round us drank all the time too. Because of the geography of the place, the TV reception was dreadful and the weather was lousy so you went to the pub. I suppose there must have been some people who wrote great opuses or worked on award-winning patchwork quilts as they holed up in their silent houses for months on end, but everyone I knew spent their waking evenings, high days and holidays, in licensed premises.

Charlie had a few inbetween times. Me too. So did Alec. And Moira.

We always had drink in the house but never sat up till all hours finishing it; never ended up so sick with drink that we ever ventured to say it was the last time.

And moreover, we were always, always happy. We talked all the time and, if we were a bit pissed the night before, we made up for it in bed in the morning.

He held my hand when we walked up the road and sometimes,

watching him working on an engine or talking to someone, I felt amazed because, no matter how engaged he looked, I knew nothing mattered more to him in the world than I did. He told me that all the time and it was true.

If there had been anything seriously amiss, surely to God I'd have sensed it?

As the local cows began to groan under the burden of unborn calves, so too did Lorraine Parker. She had ballooned from a sturdy into an enormous girl and I found her appearance quite oppressive.

I felt I was quite big enough naturally without adding to it and I winced at her engorged frontal carriage as if it were my own. Envying her was out of the question.

I met her once or twice in the company of Julia and it went as well as could be expected if you take into account that I didn't like her and her physical presence made me queasy.

Actually, envying her wasn't completely out of the question because, while having a child was something I could not contemplate, getting married was. I'd never dreamt of being a blushing bride but the ring, the commitment, the seriously grown-up nature of it appealed.

If we were married it would mean we could have big stormy rows and he couldn't just pick up his jacket and walk away. At the very least he would have to face me at the lawyers – where, of course, our eyes would meet and the passion would be rekindled.

Charlie and me didn't have rows, partly because we had nothing to argue about yet and partly because confrontations terrified me. I had this idea that, if you shouted, men left you.

Perhaps what bothered me most about the faceless Kate was that Charlie had felt strongly enough to marry her. That he had given her the luxury of being able to shout and throw things without fear of abandonment.

He hadn't done that for me and it suddenly started to matter. We'd only been together six months, so it sounds really bad, like I was one of those girls with bridalwear on the brain whereas I'd rather have spent a day mixing cement than twirling round Pronuptia.

It was the freedom of marriage I craved, the freedom to behave a bit badly and take him for granted.

I didn't really dwell on whether he'd leave me. I couldn't, it destroyed me. The prospect of life without Charlie was like life without two hands. Or eyesight.

But he didn't ask me to marry him and I wanted to know why not.

It was the evening of my nineteenth birthday and he'd driven me out to a town on the mainland, about thirty miles from home. The crossing was nauseous and the journey thereafter was through the bleakest, rainiest landscape, like something from a murder story. But as we left the sea further and further behind the road began to dry up and the sky above us broke through the cloud.

The town suddenly appeared as a belt of bright lights, shining from low houses and tall hotels, around a dark, oval loch.

We were staying the night in a hotel, which was a new thing for us. The last dirty stop-out we'd had was that awful night at Alec's. I didn't even want to think about it.

The hotel Charlie had chosen was whitewashed and sober-looking. Inside it glimmered with glassware and polished brass while a black and white collie dog bumped up and down the hall showing us his tongue and rearing his front paws like a heraldic unicorn.

Upstairs, I lay down on our bed, which was reassuringly lumpy and damp, but made up with thick white linen, and closed my eyes. I could smell lavender from somewhere inside the pillows.

How nice, I thought, to have a home like this, somewhere you've lived in ages.

'Do you not want to marry me?' I asked in a sleepy voice that I hoped sounded just the right note of whimsicality and lightness.

I heard him sigh but he didn't walk away. Charlie never walked away.

'You're only eighteen, no, nineteen. Isn't it a bit early to be thinking about that?' he asked, lighting a cigarette. It was nearly dark and I turned round to see his face briefly lit by the flare of the match. He looked like a gangster.

'I'm not asking about me – I'm asking about you.'

He sat down on the bed but without touching me and said, 'I'm naturally a bit hesitant about all that. It really didn't work out last time.'

My heart sank. I thought the least he could have done was say he'd love to. Even if he didn't mean it.

I said pettily, 'Well, David and me really didn't work out, did we? That doesn't mean I decided to stop having relationships, did it?'

And alright, I felt kind of silly saying it. Charlie fell down on the bed beside me, still in his jacket – the smart one with the shiny, ironed bit – and his fag still in his mouth.

'You woman of the world you,' he said, sucking in his cheeks as he inhaled.

I laughed, we went for dinner, we got drunk, we made love in the morning. It was lovely. I just began to wonder if he took me seriously or if, like many older men, he took his past more seriously than he took his present.

A week later we got a wedding invitation. John and Jennifer Parker request the pleasure of . . . to celebrate the marriage of Lorraine Lavender Lily (Lavender Lily!) and David Donald Gunn etc. on a tiny card the size of a box of Swan Vestas, the lettering in far too many colours for such a small space.

'Who'd have thought it, I mean, really? David, of all of them, being the first to go?' said Julia, ordering a diet coke with her vodka. She was on a diet for the wedding. 'Like it mattered,' she'd said, rolling her eyes.

'I know, I'm a bit baffled too,' I admitted, remembering David's inability to commit to holding my hand all the way across the floor of the pub, never mind a lifetime of devotion and dinner services.

'What about you and Charlie?' she asked.

'Oh, us?' I said, with a tad too much pathos, 'I doubt we'll ever do anything like that.'

'No, I doubt it too. It's just not your style.'

I made to protest but Julia, now on her second vodka, waved her arm dismissively and continued.

'You know, you two are like the only two people having a real relationship round here,' she said rather loudly.

'I . . .' Actually I rather liked the sound of that. It was just the delivery. She didn't half get stroppy on a drink these days.

'I see you two in the pub together and the rest of the world might as well not be there, and then I look at me and Bob and I just thank God the rest of the world bloody well is there or I'd fucking die of boredom,' she continued, addressing her drink.

She took several furious sips from it and continued, 'Honestly, Karen. I'm so jealous sometimes, you don't deserve it, oh God, you know what I mean. The way he looks at you compared to Bob, it's like going for a drink with my little brother. Actually Darren's probably a better kisser.'

'Julia?'

'Oh what? Oh sorry, I'm kinda pissed, I haven't eaten anything since breakfast.'

'It's not that bad, is it?'

'What? Oh Bob? Yeah . . . no, oh who cares, it's your round.'

'But you're not finished.'

'I will be by the time you get back. Look, there's a queue.'

As it happened, Julia and me didn't get the chance to talk about it any more.

Suzanna, practically unseen since the advent of Daniel Mac-Murran, her dolt of a fella, had arrived. Like many's a lady of the parish, she appeared to have contracted bridal fever and it caused her to suddenly crave female company again. All the better for discussing the bale of Butterick bridesmaid patterns spilling out from under her arm, I suspected.

'Help me,' she pleaded, running her hand over her hair in a gesture that was supposed to look helpless but just looked self-important.

I couldn't think of anything I had less enthusiasm for than looking at badly executed drawings of children wearing A-line dresses with ruff collars whilst discussing what the girl who nicked my last boyfriend was going to wear to her wedding to him.

But Suzanna was relentless. Her mental dullness often had the effect of stupifying the company, you found yourself nodding along, anything to stop her staring at you with that baffled, slightly cross expression that eventually boiled up into a tantrum.

Julia retaliated by getting filthily drunk and refusing all offers of food.

'Mrs Pankhurst woulda been proud of me,' she tittered, wagging her head at Suzanna's twenty-third offer of a Nachos Platter.

Later she declared, 'It doesn't matter what you choose Suze, they'll all look like dogs anyway.'

I must admit, I liked her style. Poor Julia. Everyone wanted to have it their own way with her, like she was some lapdog they all got a kick out of kicking. When she bit, they hated her for it.

Suzanna eventually walked out, but the night was over by then and Julia said she was tired even thinking about the apologies she'd have to go through in the morning.

'Why go through them at all?' I asked, probably rather incomprehensibly.

'It's alright for you. You've got Charlie and he loves you no matter what,' she said before bundling up into the car passenger seat of a very angry looking Bob. I've no idea if she heard me but I think she felt apologies were her place in life. Like she'd done something terrible and no one could get over it.

When I got home Charlie was sleeping heavily, slumped on the sofa in front of the gas fire. It was on full and the room was as hot as hell. I remember trying to wake him but he was too dozy to move so I switched off the fire, brought down some blankets, and tucked us in together.

We both woke up with cricks in our necks and mouths like ashtrays.

'Let's get married,' Charlie croaked and we both emitted feeble laughs.

That, I think, was the only time he ever asked me.

21

O ne thing I'll say for Charlie, he didn't give a toss for public opinion.

He said people only passed judgement on others when they were dying for a bit of drama or something to get their knickers in a knot about.

It didn't matter what they said and thought because, most of the time, they didn't even mean it.

His attitude helped me enormously when it came to shaking off the traits of island insularity. But that, as they say, is another story.

Back then, I couldn't wear a T-shirt without a bra for fear someone would think me a tart and tell the others. Charlie wore what he found on the floor and said what he found on his mind.

Thus, he wasn't even slightly rattled when his brother Alistair, who by dint of marrying David's mum Louise was therefore the stupid bastard's stepdad, effectively excluded him from all family events. David was getting married and Charlie might as well have been an old friend of his former schoolteacher's for all his involvement.

He wasn't hurt and he didn't care that people kept making remarks about it.

'Alistair has his life and I have mine,' he said simply when someone, usually my mother actually, asked why he didn't go up there and give Alistair a piece of his mind for being so neglectful of his own kin.

Mum had, all of a sudden, started taking Charlie's side in things. It was the only way she ever expressed affection and it was easy to miss if you couldn't read the signs.

'I hate all that fucking fuss before a wedding anyway,' Charlie told me. 'Everyone pissed and furious for months on end.'

He was drying a mug with a tea-towel as a labour-saving way of cleaning it. The crunchy brown disc of sugar at the bottom finally came loose and broke up all over the towel. Charlie screwed up his face, I don't know whether because of the sugar or the wedding.

He went on, 'The only one who gets anything out of it is the minister and that's only because the church is busy enough to justify putting the heating on.'

I guess. But I was curious. I took the towel and shook it out over the sink. The sugar falling on the stainless steel made a noise like sand.

'Weren't you ever close?'

'Nope. Well, as wee boys, you know, a bit.'

'So what happened? Did you fall out?'

It took me a while. Charlie was a whizz at skating across a subject and onto another one. Because his conversational pull was so irresistible I tended to be led.

He reluctantly explained that, after his mother's suicide, Alistair went to live with his dad's sister. He was only five and they never spent much time together again. Charlie, meanwhile, stayed with his dad.

I didn't quite get it. Charlie's childhood was so vague to me. He didn't even have the requisite black and white snap of two crew-cut boys grimacing into sunlight.

Charlie made a half-hearted attempt to fill in the gaps.

'Marion couldn't take both of us and Dad couldn't cope with either of us. At least I was old enough to look after myself.'

'You were only twelve, Charlie.'

'I was old enough.'

What else happened? Alistair was at Charlie's wedding, but not as best man.

He bought them a Wedgwood vase which Kate threw down the stairs, presumably shortly before she and Charlie split, when she decamped to Alistair and Louise's house for a while. Louise had gone to school with Kate and they were closer than sisters, according to Louise, who didn't have any sisters.

'Didn't that mean you and Alistair saw each other a lot then?' I asked, picturing the four of them, in a glorious flush of youth, gliding through cornfields with a picnic hamper between them and a red kite fluttering against the sky. I couldn't think of Kate without thinking of vivid colours.

'No,' he said, and he made it sound like a book being snapped shut.

But he did go to the stag-night, which promised to be a long drunken haul to hell and back.

For my sins, mainly the sin of bloody-minded nosiness, I joined the girls for the hen night. It wasn't the traditional tour of pubs due to the bride-to-be's delicate condition, though she looked far from delicate by that stage. Moreover, her wedding dress needed last-minute altering because her body had made a last-minute spurt in growth.

Lorraine lived with her granny in one of the council houses behind the village. Her mum and dad had gone out to work in Dubai a year back and weren't due in till the early hours of the following morning.

'I wonder what they'll bring you,' Suzanna kept saying, her eyes lighting up like a blackbird who's seen a glacé cherry on the bird table.

Lorraine's granny, whom everyone addressed as Granny, was a beady little creature with very thin legs. She never smiled but nonetheless gave off an air of infinite kindliness, like a noble goblin. You occasionally heard certain women making snide remarks about her, all dressed up as concern, because she bought her clothes at jumble sales. Having said that, she was no more badly dressed than anyone else.

114

When she opened the door that night to Julia and me, our Haddows bags clinking self-consciously by our sides, she frowned her welcoming frown and let us in by dint of opening the door just wide enough to allow us to squeeze through sideways.

From the outside the house was a miserably grey, rain-stained semi, just like all the others that gathered round the litter-spattered green. Inside, it was like a magpie's treasure trove, every nook and cranny twinkling with what I presumed were Granny's little finds.

Alone, how she must have clucked over her array of shiny horse-brasses and hat-pins and walking sticks! Happy Granny!

'You're here then,' said Suzanna indistinctly as we reached the living-room where she stood officiously by Lorraine's side, a fan of dress-making pins emanating from her mouth.

Lorraine beamed at us and I realised a gushing compliment was in order.

'What a beautiful dress,' I sang out, insincere as a polecat.

It actually was a beautiful dress, made of thick creamy silk with an exquisitely fashioned bodice and a long full skirt. The only problem was Lorraine. She looked as if she had stuffed a pillow inside it with her.

'Gorgeous,' echoed Julia.

But Granny simply tutted and impatiently brushed Suzanna aside.

'You look enormous, dolly,' she said, turning Lorraine around and tugging at the lower hem. Lorraine, inexplicably, continued to beam.

'You'll manage,' she said.

'You watch and see,' said Lea, who had been sitting so quietly and tinily in an enormous armchair that I had completely failed to see her. Her face wore a conspiratorial smile and I got the distinct sense that a miracle of the dress-making art was about to be enacted.

Excellent, I thought. I wasn't a particularly dressy girl, mainly because I didn't look too swell in them, but I was truly fascinated by the prospect of this wizened old lady turning Lorraine into a fairytale bride by midnight.

As Granny began to tweak fiercely at the dress, ripping out seams and pinning and folding like a fury, Lea danced into the kitchen and returned with a tray of glasses and a corkscrew.

'Whatcha got?' she asked, burrowing into our bags.

An hour later our numbers had swelled to the teens. A couple of Granny's elderly lady friends had chanced by and were now settled into the sofa with half-pints of sherry, while the younger faction sprawled across the remaining furniture and down onto the floor.

Julia, as was her wont these days, was holding forth about various matters and arguing with Suzanna who was still smarting from her summary dismissal by Granny.

Lorraine had just been released from her dress and was bundled up in a fluffy terry-towelling bathrobe. Her aged grandparent was bent double over her work, like Rumpelstiltskin in a shabby tweed skirt, and had no time to talk.

Lorraine swigged from a pint-glass of orange squash and smiled at me suddenly.

'Karen? Karen, you don't mind about me and David do you?'

'It's a bit late now if she does, eh?' hollered Julia to a stony audience.

I lit a cigarette, dallying for a second in the room's full attention, before saying with overflowing magnanimity, 'Of course I don't. Some things are just meant to be, you know?'

Don't be fooled, I couldn't have cared less. When I'd been getting changed to come out that night, standing in my knickers applying eyeliner in the bedroom mirror, Charlie had come up behind me, putting his arms round my waist and nuzzling my neck.

'You smell like a boozer,' I'd said.

'I am a boozer,' he'd replied as I helped him out of his shirt.

But Lorraine's beam grew larger, like a waxing candle about to overflow, and Lea breathed about how lovely it all was. I even earned a tiny, tight smile from Granny who paused mid-stitch without looking up, and I swelled like a loaf left rising by the fire.

*   *   *

116

An hour later our numbers had swelled to the twenties. Female visitors from all the generations, there were even a couple of pre-teens, lined the walls and covered the floors and the glasses tinkled and glimmered like a big night out at the Folies Bergères.

Lorraine had been in and out of her dress a couple of times and this time hadn't bothered with the dressing-gown at all. The heat in the room was probably about as much as she could bear and she sat there sleepily smiling in her bra and knickers, her swollen belly on parade.

One of the pre-teens, a precious little girl of about seven years old, wearing a very formal looking party dress, kept staring at it. She shuffled nearer and nearer and finally asked Lorraine, in a voice so infused with politeness it almost made you warm to the idea of having children, if it hurt.

Lorraine shook her head wearily and some haggard crone in the corner said spitefully that it would soon enough.

Julia had become seriously maudlin, and lay with her arm propped on my knee, drinking deep of the potato or whatever it is they make extra-strength vodka from.

'I'm s'fuckinfed'p,' she burped.

I said something helpful like 'oh dear' and discovered that one of the old ladies had absconded from the sofa and settled on the arm of my chair.

'You're Charlie's girl, aren't you?' she asked.

'Yes.' I had no idea who she was. She looked about sixty or so and wore cheap catalogue clothes made predominantly of crim-plene. I'm not being a snob here, I knew my catalogue clothes, having worn them all my school days.

'How is he?' she asked and I said he was good.

'I knew his mother. I'm Marion, by the way, I don't know if he's ever mentioned me.'

Of course I knew her. Alistair's supply mother.

'He found her you know. She did it the worst way. I sometimes think she meant it that way. So that George, that was Charlie's dad, would find her.' She was talking to me like I was about five years old, in a Play School kind of voice. I didn't notice at first but once I did, I paid more attention to that than what she said with it.

I put my hand on her forearm because it seemed like the thing to do and she clutched at it. Her fingers were cold leather gloves and I could feel her wedding band pressing into my fingers.

She said, without looking up, 'It was Charlie, wee Charlie, who found her.'

'I thought she . . . was it an overdose she took?' I asked. For a second I wasn't too sure we were talking about the same Charlie.

'No love, no no,' she said, shaking her head at her lap. 'She cut her wrists open in the bath and wee Charlie was the one who found her.'

This wee Charlie of hers, did Kate know all about him? Shameful as it is to relate, my initial reaction was one of jealousy – that Kate, his older, former wife who'd been around longer and earlier, might have known all this and I definitely didn't. Because I didn't matter, or couldn't be trusted, or was too young and silly.

'. . . wee soul, he was trying to be so grown up. He locked Ali in the bedroom so he wouldn't see.'

With her eyes fixed on our interlocking hands, she gave mine a squeeze. I wanted her to go away and hoped my lack of response would encourage her in this. It didn't.

'He wouldn't leave his dad. I kept saying to him, Charlie, just stay with us, but he wouldn't leave him.'

'How was his dad?' I asked, thinking of that frank fellow who said it was a relief, all in all. At least I knew something about him.

Marion made a noise, a sad little snort and gave my hand another squeeze.

Maybe not then.

'I'm glad you're there. I know you make him happy. I've seen him and he looks the best I've seen him.'

And she gave me a little smile and was gone, leaving me feeling very troubled and uncomfortable with myself. Something about Charlie's mother's suicide made me feel threatened. I wished I was with him but, even if I left now, I wouldn't find him. He'd be seriously drunk and God knows where by now.

But she'd said he was the best she'd seen him. That meant I wasn't an emotional lightweight after all. Or at least, I hoped it did.

*   *   *

118

The miracle occurred around three in the morning. Those of us still standing had drunk ourselves into a hazy sobriety and were able to appreciate it, if in a very tired way.

Somehow Granny had tailored the dress so that it clung to Lorraine's fulsome upper arms and even fuller bosom, but fell across her belly in voluptuous folds.

In place of the shotgun bride about to drop any minute was a graceful woman, the very image of fertility and beauty.

'Told you so,' simpered Lea, who was curled up in her chair like a kitten in a teacup.

'Got to hand it to your gran,' I mumbled from deep within my chair, as I let my eyes do what they'd been dying to do for about two hours, and shut down for the night.

I was woken at seven by a frantically hungover Julia.

'Hurry up,' she said, 'We've got a wedding to go to.'

22

I t was cool and bright outside after the suffocatingly orange fug of Granny's living-room. The sun was the colour of butter and the trees had turned a sudden green overnight.

We walked home in this silky dawn light, accompanied by the unholy shrilling of invisible birds, and I was so tired I felt I was literally flinging one leg in front of the other and hoping for a steady landing. Clob, clob, clob, I seemed to go, a giant ungainly monster following its fiendish master, crushing apartment complexes with every big metal step.

Julia trotted along unsteadily by my side like a pony that's taken a knock to the head, and we said goodbye at my door. She had another mile to walk, poor thing. I had visions of her holed up in a hedge some few minutes along the way, like a comely country wench who'd imbibed a flagon of cider. I would have walked her further but I was guaranteed to fall in a ditch, probably dragging her with me.

Charlie was in and wide awake. He was sitting at the kitchen table, his face and now rather shaggy hair obscured by a shaft of low sunlight.

'Hey,' he said, getting up to kiss me and then hold me at arms' length and regard me. I wondered if some sixth sense had told him about Marion's conversation with me. Or was he worried about the wedding, and what the sight of David getting married might do to my hormones?

I never found out because he suddenly burped rather biliously and I made a 'fnrrt' type noise by way of a laugh and tut combined and he hugged me. I nearly fell asleep on his shoulder.

We slept for a couple of hours. It would have been more but I set the house a-trembling to the sound of my retching in the bathroom. I think every drink I'd had the night before came up in reverse order and I was shivering with cold.

Despite my indisposition, I meant to ask Charlie about what Marion had said but I knew I couldn't give it the attention it begged because my head was swimming and all I wanted to do was lie down on the floor. Anyway, the morning of a wedding was hardly the time.

I remember Charlie having a little smile to himself as he murmured what a pitiful sight I made while he wrapped a blanket round my naked shoulders and helped me back to bed.

Eventually I entered the out-of-danger zone and was able to get out of bed and bump around the room looking for my clothes.

'Don't let me get too pissed,' I said, noting that I still sounded like a second-rate comedian pretending to be blotto. I pinned a yellow rose over the shiny patch on Charlie's jacket lapel and noticed the violent pinkness of his eyes. I pointed this out.

'It's hay fever,' he insisted, suppressing another burp.

I did like him in that suit. It made him look shambling and constrained and as if he'd be much happier out of it, which was just how I wanted him.

I wore a red dress. I wasn't too sure if red was an appropriate colour for a wedding but it seemed appropriate for us.

Red for passion, wine and broken thread veins.

And it sat well on me, if I say so myself. Because so few things did, when it happened my whole appearance rose to the occasion. My body was like an old lady in a smoky Salford tenement – it didn't have many days in the sun. But it made the most of it when it did. I suddenly got taller – though I hardly needed to, I was almost taller than Charlie as it was – and inexplicably slimmer. And my hair turned out glossy, with all the split ends neatly tucked away, and my skin looked like finest porcelain as opposed to that lumpy clay they make mugs out of.

'You'll do fine,' said Charlie, attempting to look smouldering but actually looking as if his pockets were on fire and he was too dazed to notice.

Like all weddings round there, David and Lorraine's began with long, giggly hellos and a service and, almost on a sixpence, turned into a rammy of shouting and drinks.

The service was brief and inaudible and everyone seemed to be preoccupied with chewing something or playing with their false teeth.

David, whose hair had been cut so short he looked about fourteen years old, looked round and winked at us both. I felt like I was watching a wee brother win a trophy at Scouts rather than a man who had tired of having sex with me marry someone he wasn't quite so tired of.

The Royal Stuart hosted the reception but even when swamped with white clothed tables and flowers up to the rafters, it still looked like the kind of place you were guaranteed a good fight in.

It had been the place where the older generation met with the travelling dentist, the one who pulled all your teeth out as a seventeenth birthday, coming-of-age treat. Then they'd drink away the pain while blood from their gums dribbled onto the lapels of the newest suit they'd ever own.

It had always been the place where you celebrated, even if what you were celebrating was actually disfigurement and agony.

That day could as easily have been a wake or the visit of a faith healer, there were as many people weeping and a-wailing as there were cheering.

Lorraine had been wearing cream-coloured carnations in her hair and, by the time the cake was being cut, Jocky was wearing them.

He spent the evening trying to take advantage of being best man by relentlessly pursuing the prettiest bridesmaid, who could have been anything between fifteen and thirty-five years old.

He tore past me, hot and red with drink, his flowers dangling precariously over his ears. Instinctively I tucked one of them back and he shouted 'cheers' over his shoulder, not realising who had tidied him up. When he did, he stopped briefly in his tracks and smiled sweetly. I know this sounds like my mother, but he really was a dear boy.

Charlie was with me all evening and a crowd of the heavier, if less boisterous, drinkers gathered round us, drawn to the magnet of our – comparatively speaking – glamour.

In a way, I was glad of the company because I would have started some heavy conversation with Charlie and it might have gone terribly wrong if I'd gotten a bee in my bonnet about his intimacy with Kate.

And then, surprise of surprises, David asked me to dance. Perhaps it was his shiny new wedding ring, but he carried with him such an air of authority and sexy new grown-upness that, for a split-second, I wondered if this should have been mine.

We danced badly, we always had done, but we talked like former lovers, which we'd never done.

What's this? I wondered, when he took my hand and led me to the door.

'I'm dying for a fag. Can't smoke in there, I'm supposed to have given up,' he said and I obligingly fished in my bag for the packet.

I asked him what it felt like to be an imminent father and he shrugged and smiled at me as he blew a huge belch of smoke into the evening air.

I told him I thought Lorraine looked wonderful and he shrugged and smiled again.

'You're not bothered, are you?' I said playfully, and he leaned over and kissed me full on the mouth. For a moment I could feel his tongue against my teeth and I darted back, muttering don'ts.

'We shouldn't be doing this,' I said, generously shouldering some of the blame for his being a sexual incontinent all of a sudden. He shrugged and smiled again and the part of my brain that got excited about boys shut down for the night. He may have had a wedding ring on his finger but he was still a git.

I'm not sure how much Charlie knew about this carry-on with David. He didn't seem to, not that there was much to know. I left his side a few times, to talk to my mother, to Julia, even to Lorraine, but he was always to be found where I left him, drink in hand, unkempt drunkards by his side.

You see, there was a follow-up. I'd gone up to the loo and, coming down, he, David, was leaning on the wall and seemed to be waiting for me.

'You look fantastic,' he said, with a lecherous gleam in his eye.

I said something tart about it being a bit late for all that now and then I asked, kind of casually but quite intrigued to know, why he married Lorraine anyway. And he said, 'Because you never asked.'

'What? And Lorraine did?' I asked, unsuccessfully trying to sidle away from him.

'She didn't need to. It was obvious.'

'And that's all it took? Someone to be obvious?' I gasped.

He shrugged. 'You know, that's how these things happen.'

I was totally nonplussed and then he leaned over, kissed my ear, and said, 'But that doesn't mean we can't go out for a drink together sometime, eh?'

Which was enough to put me off David Gunn for life. Wee brother my arse. Some prematurely fat old lech in his nineties more like.

I was also appalled by his tiny expectations for the future. He was entering marriage as lightly as he'd sally into a used car showroom, without so much as a nod to the standard Scottish minimum of six months voluntary fidelity.

But then I saw a lighter side to it all. Lorraine thought it was fair play to shag my boyfriend, did she? Well, there was a whole load of fair play coming her way now.

Neil, Charlie and me were the last to leave. We always were, come to think of it. Neil was so drunk he could barely stand so we had to take him home and tuck him into bed. It took over an hour and it was screamingly funny but, as we closed his front door behind us, Charlie said, 'He doesn't look after himself, that boy.'

And I had to laugh because here were we, two supposed adults, weaving home at dawn for the second time in twenty-four hours. He laughed too but I think he would have pipped a clockwork laughing policemen at the post for sounding hollow and insincere.

Because he was quiet on the way home I began thinking again about Marion. It seemed very surreal now, because I hadn't been sober then, or since.

When we got in I poured us both a large whisky and braced myself. Charlie looked at me questioningly, he could always tell – and I said something like 'I know about your mother' and he almost jumped out his skin.

'I mean, Marion told me. She was at Lorraine's granny's house and she came and talked to me.'

He sniffed and said that was more than she'd ever done with him, then asked, rather testily, what exactly she'd said. So I told him. And I can't say he looked happy about it. In fact, he went rather quiet and took so many swigs of whisky that he ended up pouring another before he said anything. I took a top-up too and felt my eyes following him round the room like one of those spooky portraits on *Scooby Doo*.

'That's what happened,' was all he said, sitting down and looking at the glass in his hand.

'Oh, why didn't you tell me?' I wailed and moved to sit on the arm of his chair. But he made a gesture to stop me and said, though gently enough, 'I don't really want to talk about it.'

I very nearly said, but I bet you talked to Kate about it.

He added, 'I will tell you one day, I promise I will. It's not even that I don't feel that I'm close to you, because I do. It's just that, Karen, I don't even know how.'

'Did you talk to your dad about it?'

He shook his head and I had the feeling he was actually crying and I froze.

'Charlie?'

He shook his head again and smiled up at me, 'I will tell you about it, I promise. Just not now.'

And I had to accept that. I knew that Charlie kept his promises and anyway I didn't know how to go about forcing someone to let it all out.

Nor did it hang over us – he saw to that. By the time we went to bed, which was around nine in the morning when God-fearing children were sitting down to their sums, we were talking bollocks and laughing like horses.

I don't think I got up at all the next day.

23

The knock-on effect of Lorraine and David's wedding was that every local girl under the age of seventy-five began to foam at the mouth for matrimony.

Julia cornered Bob about it – well, be fair, they had been 'dating' for going on two years – and he told her, very amusingly I'm sure, that he'd never marry anyone with a 'backside like an elephant's'.

You know, he may have been lardy, stupid and all-round contemptible but, ho, could he make you chuckle. Rather unsurprisingly, he failed to make Julia chuckle and she chucked him. I'm still amazed it wasn't on *News at Ten*, I just couldn't believe she'd finally stood up for herself.

Then the inevitable happened. The big fart forgot his condom and got a student nurse he'd met on a stag night in the family way. However, she wasn't as dazzled by that good bit of farm coming to him as might have been predicted and graciously allowed Bob to pay for her private abortion.

After hearing about it, from someone she'd never met before in the middle of the High Street, Julia marched into the Royal Stuart and slapped Bob so hard across the face it nearly set off a tidal wave in the Pacific. And that's when he delivered the only witty one-liner of his entire life.

He said, wheezing slightly, 'I'm sorry. Should I have waited till you'd had one?'

*   *   *

A few weddings did break out across the island but no one I knew, not even me. It was a subject Charlie deliberately avoided and I thought, I'll wait till we're in Spain.

The month beforehand I was preoccupied with trying to lose weight. This had been prompted by watching skinny little Charlie stand on the bathroom scales in someone else's bathroom – it was late on at a party, you didn't bother about peeing in front of your loved one by then – and noting that he weighed a stone and a half less than I did.

I outright refused to follow suit because I knew the truth.

I envisaged us as some horrible kind of caricature couple. He with a scrawny neck and spaghetti-thin bow legs and me spilling out of a giant flowery swimming costume, my calves like two boiled hams. I think, on reflection, that we actually looked very nice together but that stone and a half nearly killed me.

I tried counting calories but drinking at night always threw me right off target. So I caved in and just saved all my calories for drink. Dieters worldwide can rattle off the calories in half a banana or a baked potato but few could beat me on the respective values of Tennent's Lager as opposed to gin and slimline tonic, dry red wine or Sweetheart Stout.

It wasn't a regime that did a lot for my complexion, but it got me thin. Though I think I owed my permanently flat stomach to dehydration rather than loss of actual body fat.

My mother, like all mothers, became alarmed as soon as she discerned I was no longer at my peak of fatness.

'Is this down to Charlie?' she would ask. As if she thought he openly mocked me whilst ogling pictures of models in *Cosmopolitan*. Even I, insecure adolescent that I was, realised Charlie thought I was drop-dead gorgeous. If I'd told him about my weight gain horrors I think he would have been genuinely startled.

Charlie preoccupied himself with trying to get a passport which is how I found out he wasn't actually divorced yet.

'But you're down as my next-of-kin,' he whimpered over the storm of my verbosity.

'But why aren't you divorced? I would have thought you'd want to be,' I screamed with such vitriol it's amazing he didn't run back into her arms that very moment.

He shambled awkwardly where he stood, while I puffed myself out and finally sat down. He mumbled humbly, 'It was just something we never got round to. Because of money and, well, there was no need. We said we would if either of us had children.'

He must have seen the gleam in my eye, the one that came and went so quickly I barely registered it, because he grabbed my arm and all but shouted, 'Don't even think about that, Karen. Please, no fucking accidents.'

Which seemed a bit unnecessary, and I said so. He apologised and added, in a voice as soft as butter, 'If we're going to have a child, let's do it when the time's right.'

I remained bloody furious and nearly cancelled the holiday. But I just couldn't sustain bad feeling with Charlie, it made me think we'd split up and I'd have done just about anything to make sure that didn't happen. To be honest, I think he'd have been the same.

We left on a blindingly hot day and, because our flight was delayed, got so pissed up at the airport bar we almost missed it completely.

I fell asleep while Charlie worked his way through a series of double gins whilst staring out the window with an expression of abject terror. When we landed it was my turn to be terrified. I couldn't believe it was so hot and couldn't imagine how I would live through a fortnight of it without wanting to kill myself. I don't suppose having a horribly sweaty hangover helped much either.

We stayed in a tiny white room in a hotel that looked like a series of white building blocks piled randomly on top of each other. Every other room seemed to be occupied by radioactive north-erners with squads of children who spent entire days jumping bum-first into the hotel pool.

That first afternoon I lay down on the bed, the skin on my

shoulders and cheeks smarting from the sun, and listened to the alien sounds of shouting and splashing. The heat made my body heavy and I watched Charlie as he slung the contents of our cases into drawers and realised he looked different in this light.

People always look not quite themselves when you meet them in foreign countries; the quality of light and air changes them.

I remembered that I always hated the first day abroad, I found it too alien.

Charlie interrupted my thoughts saying, 'It's weird, isn't it?'

I nodded and got up and went into the shower, hoping to wash my hangover away. He followed me and we fumbled under the capricious little showerhead though I don't know why because we neither of us felt like it. We were both very unsettled, that was all.

Later we wandered out into the town, a perfect little crescent of twinkling lights and bobbing marinas. Behind this tiara of bars and bistros were a brace of inland sidestreets, where white houses covered in vines stood cheek by jowl with chaotic supermarkets and cafés tilting sideways onto pavements.

Our first night was nervous, what with the currency, the language and the fact that we were both really scared this whole holiday was a big mistake. Much as we tried to conceal it from each other, we might as well have been yelling it through megaphones.

Quite late, we called in at a bar that looked out onto the pitch black beach. I ordered sangria, remembering that Mum and Dad used to drink it when we came to Spain, and was surprised to discover how strong it was.

'Well, no wonder they liked it,' said Charlie. 'They needed something strong to blot out the fact that they were on holiday with each other. Och sorry, Karen, I like your mum, I really do.'

I wasn't upset by his dissing my folks – I was upset that he might think we needed sangria too.

'I'm sorry,' he said, leaning over and taking my hand. 'I've never been abroad before. I was shitting bricks coming over in that plane, but I'll be fine tomorrow. I'm fine now.'

*   *   *

129

And he was. He made me coffee, bought from the supermarket downstairs, while I was still in the bathroom, furiously trying to scrub several months' worth of nicotine off my teeth. That's the thing about bright light – it shows up faults you'd never even noticed before. Oh for the dark corners of Scotland.

Later we wandered down to the beach and I tried sunbathing but found it too boring, and tried reading but found it impossible to read books in the inhumanly bright light. Charlie was quite content to flop out on the beach for hours without end, his eyes shut and his brain, as far as I could tell, on hold.

Naturally, he turned brown overnight while I remained a stubborn yellow with pink highlights. I felt the day only really got going when, about four o'clock, we sat down in a beachside bar and ordered up a couple of beers.

The days were like that. At night, we had a drink, a shag, a shower, a sleep and then went out for dinner. And more to drink. Well, we were on holiday. It was blissfully monotonous. We meant to sightsee or take a trip but, really, there was nothing we were interested in seeing.

My lazybone came out and basked in the sun.

But it wasn't all blissful. My zeal to resolve the marital issue saw to that. I left off for the first few days but then it came upon me one night and that was it.

I didn't seem able to stop myself and Charlie's face would go tight. I felt like I was hammering away at our relationship, shaking it so hard it was starting to crack, but I couldn't stop.

'But I thought you loved me,' I would whine.

'I do fucking love you,' he would say, like he'd gladly shoot me if only it didn't mean a custodial sentence.

Invariably one or other of us got up and walked away from some white rickety table leaving half a drink behind. The next morning I would wonder to myself if I was going mad but, even then, I could feel my anger rankling like a rat in a basement.

*　　*　　*

130

One afternoon well into our second week I turned on him while I was sober.

We were sitting on the beach, squinting at each other while large youths thudded past in pursuit of a football.

I asked him again and he said, very calmly, 'It would hobble your life if you were married to me.'

'I'm not a child, you know. I can decide that for myself,' sounding about as grown-up as a recently smacked five-year-old.

'Well, it seems like you can't.'

'What?' I demanded, my anger detonating inside my chest.

Charlie looked at me wearily and studied his bronzed feet. He said, in an infuriatingly sing-song voice, 'I'm more than twice your age, I'm dead-end and I'm a drunk. My dad was a drunk, and so was his dad before him. We never amounted to anything. This,' and he threw his arm back to encapsulate the beach and the litter of white, Legoland hotels, 'is my lifetime's achievement so far.' His voice rose steeply, 'What the fuck do you want of me because, whatever it is, you're not going to get it.'

And he looked up at me with such an expression of resentment that I clumsily got to my feet, wrapped my towel round me in a helplessly pathetic gesture, and walked away. He didn't follow.

I marched back to our hotel room and lay on the bed till I fell asleep, though that took a while because I was still snorting with the panic I was trying to dress up as outrage. I wanted him to come to me and say he was sorry, or even say anything, so long as it meant we were OK. I slept really fitfully and woke up to the late afternoon in a state of dull terror. Charlie was still not back.

I knew he probably hadn't gone home – how could he? – but I didn't know where he was.

I lay for a while and then scrambled to my feet, got dressed and hurried out to the beach. The sun had burnished everything it touched. Old women with harsh skin and red raw complexions were given warmth and depth, the sand went gold and the sea a liquid indigo.

A few late sunbathers hung on but the beach belonged to couples wandering home and locals with their dogs. Certainly not to Charlie anyway. I looked up at the promenade, maybe he was watching me – but he wasn't there either.

I left the beach and kept walking until I was in the sidestreets. I passed a restaurant, a tucked-by-the-wayside little place that only real Ibizans went to. I stared at a young Spanish couple as they stared at their brown little boy who was drinking a Coca-Cola with both his chubby hands clutching the glass.

She was wearing an orange sundress like mine and she looked up at me and wrinkled her nose in a smile. I smiled back and the effort made me feel very gracious and also very sad.

I wandered into the town square and sat down on a bench facing the fountain.

Across from me an elderly Spaniard in a gleaming white shirt leaned with his arms spread across the back of his bench, looking benevolently at the people who passed by. He was very peaceful and his skin was as dry and brown as parchment and I thought, that must feel good, to be old and peaceful.

I didn't notice Charlie till he put his arm round my shoulders and I nearly smacked him across the jaw, thinking it was some randy tourist chancing his arm.

He smiled at me and I was so relieved and pleased to see him that I immediately burst into noisy tears and he stroked my hair and said everything was fine.

Which it was after that.

He took me to a café where I smoked about ten cigarettes in as many minutes and choked back several glasses of beer and tried to get back to feeling alright again.

Later, we took a bottle of wine to our room and sat on the tiny veranda overlooking shadowy streets where little boys played on bikes.

'Imagine being able to speak Spanish at that age,' Charlie said.

I told him about the French assistant who came to our primary school. I'd asked him if he could count to a hundred in French – come on, I was only six – and he'd laughed a deep brown laugh and nodded and said, 'I can count to a thousand, as a matter of fact.'

'Karen, what are you going to do?' Charlie asked all of a sudden.

'Right now, I'm going to the lavvy. As for the rest of my life, who knows?'

When I came back he was still looking at me.

'It was the rest of your life I was talking about.'

I didn't detect any danger. I thought everything was possible, that I could have it all ways.

'I'd like to, I don't know, at least not be like Lorraine or so on. You know, stuck at the sink and listening to the conversation of those old biddies who're proud of the fact they've never been further than the ferry.'

'So that's what you don't want,' he said.

So I said about the university thing, about getting some big bastard of a qualification and then I didn't really know, the way forward would be clear by then. And I said about the young Spanish couple with the kid. And all the time Charlie nodded, and he said, 'There's no reason why you can't do all of those things.'

And I said I didn't know how and we talked about how. He was surprisingly clued up about all this stuff, about how to sit Highers and about getting a grant and what courses there were.

'I've always fancied the idea of working for the World Service,' I said, to my own surprise. But it seemed perfect in this exotic location to want to see the whole damn shooting match, to voice the news, the big serious history-making stuff, to the globe.

'You'd better do languages then,' he said.

'Oh, I can't do languages,' I snorted.

'How do you know? Come on, when did you last even try? Don't tell me, when you were sitting in school with Julia, staring out the window?'

I giggled. He was absolutely right. I'd never tried to do anything.

'You've got to try Karen. You only get one life and you're wasted where you are.'

I went to sleep that night with a head buzzing full of possibilities. Charlie was quiet and said he was just really tired.

'I find fighting on the beach most exhausting,' he grinned.

I didn't even think about the fact that, all the time we were talking, we only talked about me.

24

When we got back we were smugly informed that we'd wasted our money going abroad because there had been a heatwave in Scotland. It certainly looked that way because everyone had turned maple-coloured and the Drumclair had even made use of its all but redundant beer garden.

I wished we hadn't gone though I couldn't quite put my finger on why. Charlie was still as loving as ever but I felt that we'd sustained some kind of damage.

And I felt like it was down to me, that I'd done something, gone too far with the marriage thing, I don't know.

I said this to Charlie and he grabbed me and said it was fine, we were alright.

'Aren't we?' he said, looking at me with his deep, dark eyes and making me want to cry, though why I didn't know.

It was nearly a year since I'd been ditched by David and I couldn't think about it without feeling terribly sad. Not because of David but because, twelve months ago, I was just about to meet and fall in love with Charlie. That sounds a bit strange but I felt that something awful was about to happen and it was breaking my heart.

Late summer evenings are melancholy enough without the infusion of impending tragedy.

Julia kept bending my ear about her situation with Bob. They'd got back together, more from lack of options than anything else I think, and he was still behaving like a shite.

Worse than before by the sounds of it. He seemed almost chuffed with himself about his slip-up with the nurse and Julia was getting her nose well and truly rubbed in it. And all I could think about, while listening to her, was how simple and clear-cut her situation was compared to mine. Mine was intangible and Charlie denied it was there, but I felt it all the same.

I went back to school, pretty much on his insistence, to sit Highers in French and English. It was horrendous because I had to sit in a classroom full of schoolkids who stared at me over their shoulders and tittered constantly. I was forever checking that my nose wasn't a veritable Fingal's Cave of dried snot or my bra-straps weren't in full view.

I came home the first day and told Charlie categorically that I was never going back.

He laughed, saying, 'Don't be such a tit.' And then set me down to read the first three chapters of *A Farewell to* bloody *Arms* while he made the dinner.

'I'd rather be in the pub,' I said.

'You can do that later,' he sang gaily from the kitchen.

But even in the pub he was subdued. I felt there were long silences where there hadn't been before. We, who'd never been stuck for things to say to each other, suddenly couldn't find words. And when I'd run out of things to say to boyfriends before, that was it, we were history.

I chattered about Julia, blithely divulging her secrets in a bid to engage his interest and he listened patiently without showing a hint of interest.

'She's a silly girl,' was all he'd say.

'But what can she do?'

'She could do what you're doing. She doesn't need to settle for him.'

One night I asked him, 'Have you ever read Hemingway?'

He raised his eyebrows at this. 'Of course. I went to school too, you know.'

'Did you do sixth year?' I asked in surprise and he nodded, with a wry little smile on his face.

'Did you?' I said again, my jaw so dropped you could have inserted golf-balls between my teeth.

'Ye-es,' he repeated patiently, with a mock-offended expression on his face.

'Ach,' he said, snatching my A4 pad off the chair to sit down, 'I did intend to do something like you're doing because I didn't fancy ending up like my dad.'

'Was he that bad?'

'He wasn't that unusual, there's loads of men like him. Lazy and nothing to say for themselves and he had such a shitty job, and got practically bog-all for doing it.'

'What did he do?'

And Charlie laughed, with a gentle undertow of bitterness, 'He was a mechanic. Just like me.'

Oh fuck. I wasn't enjoying this turn in the conversation.

'But you're not like him?'

'How would you know?' and he looked at me intently.

I was on my way to work one morning and was met by Mary, who was walking up the road to find me.

'Go see your mum,' she said and I broke into a run thinking I'd find her collapsed at the bottom of the stairs, her bony white hands clutching an empty paracetemol bottle.

Which she wasn't, but her eyes were red and sore from crying. It looked like she had conjunctivitis and her skin was covered in raw patches where eczema had broken out.

'What the hell is the matter with you?' I asked, flailing for the kettle.

She blew her nose and sniffed loudly, retracting what sounded like rivers of mucus up her sinuses.

In contrast to which, her voice sounded very genteel. She said, 'I know it looks bad but I've done something I'm really very proud of.'

'What have you done then missus?'

She sniffed again, 'I've broken off with my boyfriend. He was,

I'm afraid to say, married (and here she nodded curtly at the floor) and I shouldn't have had any part of it. After all, I know exactly what it bloody well (speeding up here) feels like and it's not nice.'

I was amazed, once again, that she thought she'd kept the identity of her boyfriend a secret from me. What did she think? That I thought Frankie McAllister chuffed into our holiday park for the good of his health? And that she just went for long, days-long walks?

'Is this a congratulations situation?' I wondered, switching on the kettle again even though it had just boiled. I'd already had two pots of tea that morning and had no enthusiasm for bringing closure to this task.

'Your father was a swine and so was this man. It's taken me a long time to realise this.'

'Did that Mary put you up to this?' I said and we both had a shaky giggle.

Mary, I was beginning to realise, was worth her weight in gold and, believe me folks, that was a lot of gold. Somehow this elderly matron, who laboured Sisyphus-like the day long, had located the deep trough wherein my mother had long ago buried her self-respect, and dusted it off.

It was more than the proprietor of the Royal Stuart had ever been able to do.

I guess, in the grand scheme of things, it didn't make much difference. My mum was still a scrawny little lady who lived on benefits and was pathologically afraid of going outside on her own, but it was still something that she'd chosen to quit being someone's mistress out of respect for his wife. And herself. It really was something.

I eventually made that tea and she told me that, when Dad walked out, she'd felt like she deserved it. I wondered why and she said it was because of her mother not being married.

'There weren't things like therapy in those days. She didn't know that blaming me for everything made me blame myself for everything.'

*   *   *

137

I hadn't ever noticed that my gran, that frosty-faced old baggage who never gave me sweets – even though that's what grand-parents are for, for heaven's sake – had been unmarried. I'd assumed there'd been some Stan Ogden-type grandad who'd popped his slippers back in the fifties. I'd never asked of course, but then, children tend to be disappointingly uncurious about their heritage.

'Poor old bag,' I said idly.

Mum nodded, 'Yes, I suppose she was.'

'No, I meant you.'

And she found that funny enough to nearly swallow her cigarette.

I told her about my Higher classes as I was leaving to go downstairs and she hugged me tight.

'Good times are coming,' she said, sounding like Judy Garland in *The Wizard of Oz*.

In fact, I soon began to feel that they were. Charlie remained that bit quieter but we still had enough 'I love you' moments to reassure me.

I discovered to my delight that, when it came to Higher English, I was actually a bit of a star. My Higher French got put on hold because, quite frankly, I was completely chronic at it.

My English teacher was a nice enough woman from Edin-burgh who had a habit of tugging her jumper down over her hips before speaking, and she would raise her brows archly when handing me back my work.

'That was well done, Karen.'

I didn't even flinch the way I would have done a couple of years before. I didn't give a toss if all those mascara'd beauty queens thought I was a swotty dotty sad girl because I didn't have to hang out with them at playtime. When my classes were done I could bugger off to the pub if I wanted. Which I sometimes did if Charlie or Julia were around.

Actually, Charlie started to get quite into what I was doing. He'd read my essays, tut over my spelling and ask about my reading. He even started doing some reading himself.

'It's the life, innit?' he'd say over a copy of Hemingway short stories, 'Fishing, looking at logs and eating apple butter, eh?'

'Why don't you sit the Higher too?' I asked, picturing us together at the back of the classroom, a ludicrous pair of charlies craning over our tatty reading books. Maybe he conjured up the same vision because he just grunted and said, 'No way. This is your thing.'

But it didn't stop him turning into a right curmudgeon when it came to grammar. Particularly superfluous inverted commas which seemed to be coming into vogue at that time.

'I mean, why have them round soup of the day?' he'd shout into a mid-morning silence, tweaking his fingers to indicate the offending little punctuation marks.

'Is it not really soup of the day but . . . something, nudge, nudge, else? Is "soup of the day", perchance, doublespeak for "we rent rooms by the hour, if you know what I mean"?'

I ruffled his hair.

'Is this what happens when you get old?' I asked sweetly.

And then Lorraine had her baby. It was born at five minutes to midnight on the first of October.

I first met Marianne Elizabeth Gunn on the 14th and was delighted with her, which is more than I can say for the mother who appeared to hate the little thing.

'She's got post-natal depression,' David told me as he slipped his daughter into my arms. Judging by the black smudges under his eyes and the ashen colour of his skin, he had radiation sickness. I'd never seen him look so dreadful.

Marianne liked Charlie. He seemed to instinctively know how to hold babies and she gurgled with pleasure at being in such capable hands.

'What will you do?' I asked David as he screwed the top on a milk bottle.

'I don't know. We'll manage,' and he emitted a pitifully brave smile.

We didn't know it then but David and Marianne were destined to manage pretty much alone. Lorraine got better sometimes and

139

then sank back into what wasn't really post-natal depression, just depression.

I felt very guilty about it for a long time, thinking that my bad wishes had made it happen. Charlie told me to stop being such an arsehole and he was right.

She was a poor, tragic cow. It was nobody's fault.

25

I often think they got it wrong, the Christians and the pagans, when it came to autumn. I feel it should have been the beginning of the year, not the second last season.

Like a birthday, it's an annual marker in your life. Most times there is some idea there of making a new start or going off in a new direction.

But you don't start off brand new. First, you have to shed all the old you, all the bits you don't want any more.

Like if you're leaving your marriage, you have to pack your bags and do all that crying and see your solicitor. That's autumn, you see, when you're peeling off the old stuff and letting it fall around your feet like leaves.

Then comes the winter, when you really have to get your head down and get on with it. Beginnings are always hard, there's always that bleak patch where you're no further forward and you seem to fall flat on your face with every step. The only thing sustaining you is the conviction that change will come.

Which it does, in spring. Things start to bear fruit and you're motivated to keep going. The world is kinder and softer and you've reached somewhere new. And then comes summer, like a big cake that you've baked all by yourself. It's an achievement, all those leaves and flowers and the heavy scent of grass turning into hay. That's when you see how far you've come.

Only the academics got it right. Those dusty people hidden

behind words. Autumn is the start. It's the time when you open up the books and see what you're in for.

Autumn found me deep in books, which seemed apt. Hemingway was deeply tedious really, I would never read him now, but I was quietly thrilled to be covering sides of A4 with inky theses on symbolism and a lack of adjectives.

There was poetry too. I read about a boy who was taken from his class mid-term and informed of his brother's death, and Norman McCaig's visit to a geriatric ward, and Philip Larkin's arrows somewhere becoming rain.

It's all dog-eared, Wednesday afternoon stuff but it was new to me then and I saw it as a connecting corridor to the future. Though I had no idea what form the future would take, feeling it tug me forward made me feel suddenly very alive. As if I'd been asleep for years or somehow not quite myself.

Julia was impressed when she saw my dedication. She kept rolling her eyes and saying she just didn't have it in her. I told her she'd never tried and she agreed.

'I know,' she said, 'but what difference would it make? I'm just going to get married and have kids anyway.'

Who's that talking? I wondered. Her mother? Bob?

I used to wonder too what Corrie would have been like if she has still been alive. I liked to think of her as a slightly stout, bossy redhead catching the morning bus to college.

Of course, she might have become a serial shagger with squads of children, all by different fathers, and a Buckfast habit. But I preferred to think of us as two clever little peas in a pod, being unbearably smug together as we boarded the bus to St Andrews. Which would be full of good-looking young men, of course.

But I had the smile wiped off my face one day. I'd been particularly know-all during a lesson – I'd long since lost my nervousness about talking up in class – and a girl in front of me, Shona MacKay, flicked her hair disdainfully and said, 'It's pretty easy stuff if you're only doing the one class all year.'

I waddled home miserably and told Charlie all about it, hoping he would agree that Shona was a right tart.

Instead he said, 'She's right. You should do something else. You've got the time and you're obviously good at learning.'

I said, how could I? I'd already proved I couldn't do French.

'Ah, that's right. All those nights you sat up till dawn conjugating verbs and you just *couldn't*. I'm telling you, there wasn't a dry eye in the house.'

'You think I should do French, don't you?'

He nodded. Damn him.

So I approached the French teacher again. He was a large man with slicked back, jet black hair and a dangerously dark red skin tone. 'Stop eating salt,' I wanted to say, but couldn't think how to fit it into our exchange.

His name was something like Arthur Donald, but he was referred to as Monsieur Donald which sounded ridiculous, that long, elongated 'mi-sure' capped off with the two dead beats of 'Donald'. Only lanky wags in sixth year dared to say 'Donaald'.

He drummed his corpulent fingers on his register and smiled smugly at his legs, which were crossed daintily despite their girth.

'And why do you want to do this?' he asked, smiling the smile of an art gallery visitor smirking at a Magritte because, oh yes, he *got* the visual joke.

'Because I've discovered that I can learn. And I know I've missed an awful lot,' I said, managing to sound both pompous and grovelling all at the same time, 'but I'm willing to put in the time to catch up.'

'Oh,' and he sat up. 'Oh, well, ehm, start on Friday. It's language lab.'

Ugh. He might as well have said naked hockey in the rain.

'Excellent,' I lied, as he handed me a series of dismal, tatty books featuring Jean-Paul and his sister Françoise, whose hair stood out from the back of her head like a blancmange.

French wasn't easy, but it wasn't hell either. I got by, mainly because my vocabulary just about compensated for the tangle of

143

pluperfects and modals and whatever else that cluttered my learning passages like so many pollen spores.

I didn't see a future at the European Parliament but I could just about smell a C pass if I really crammed at the end.

I did fewer days at the café but still got paid the same, which I guess must have been down to Mary. Even when I was there she encouraged me to take half hour breaks and 'sit down with your books, I'll bring you a roll.'

I didn't, God forgive me, visit my mother often. I preferred to think of her as a benign presence looking out for me.

Despite our big breakthrough we still managed, for the most part, to have silly, narky conversations about how I needed to wash my hair more often.

Charlie and I kind of lived side by side during the weeks. He'd go to work and I'd stay home, minding my studies as he used to say. I was very preoccupied with what I was doing and, I think, must have been a bit of a bore about it sometimes. The poor sod had to listen to me babbling like a schoolgirl about the fact that, indeed, I had become a schoolgirl.

'Do you want to read my essay?' I'd say and he would wag his head brightly and wade through my almost illegible handwriting, exclaiming about how good it all was.

But after the first few weeks, it didn't really matter if he thought it was good because I knew it was. He didn't need to hold my hand for long and, brave man, he didn't keep clinging when I started to let go.

I suppose it must have been a bit grim for him, being suddenly relegated to the sidelines, listening to me going on and on and on.

He never said.

26

I started drinking seriously when I was eighteen and I'd left it later than most.

Once I started, I couldn't understand why I'd never done it before. It made me funnier, more articulate and it stopped me being afraid. If only, I sometimes thought, I could be pissed all the time.

But it made me look like crap and that, rather than anything else, bothered me. I'd lay off for a few days every once in a while and let my complexion return to something approaching normal.

Charlie, well, I knew Charlie hit the bottle hard but I never saw a problem with it. He never had shaky hands, or developed a red nose cross-hatched with thread veins. He was never sick or out of control and he always got up the next morning. I didn't see a problem and, more significantly, nor did he. Because he was older and supposedly wiser, I trusted his instincts.

We had some hilarious times, if a bit surreal. We got into a habit of working fairly soberly through the weekdays and letting it all go to hell at the weekends.

Sometimes the weeks seemed so long we anticipated Friday with a Thursday night batter, or even a Wednesday night. Come to think of it, there were weekends that started on a Monday, but they were the exception.

Sometimes I don't really remember how they started. Once it began with a letter about Help the Aged. I must have had a few glasses of something already because it had a profound effect upon me. I was almost in tears about frail old women without the means to heat their sitting-rooms and I wanted Charlie to understand how terrible this was and share my pain.

He was slumped on the sofa reading something from the local paper, probably a bit fed up listening to me, and I was pouring out an extra measure of whisky for each of us, using the kind of exaggerated slow movements employed by Tom when sneaking up on Jerry. Had there been anyone sober in the room, I'm sure I would have been spotted but evidently there wasn't. Charlie appeared oblivious to his drink being enlarged. Either that or he was quite happy about it or he could very well have said no for all I remember.

Soon we were talking animatedly in that 'hurray!' kind of way when the drink starts to speed you up and make your brain go into overdrive. The ashtray had turned into a First World War battlefield of brown stumps and grey mud and the whisky level was nearing the bottom of the bottle.

I was clumsily applying mascara in the bathroom mirror while Charlie held the front door open, waiting for me.

There was the bar of the Royal Stuart, and I couldn't find Charlie at all. Julia's brother Darren helped me to my feet and told me I was fine and I started crying because I didn't know where Charlie had gone and he said he'd go and find him for me.

A long walk in the rain. Bloody endless. Rain.

Someone's house. I'd dropped a glass and someone was picking up the shards and putting them in a wastepaper basket. His hands were cut to ribbons. It might have been Charlie.

I was listening to a guy about my age telling me that his fiancée had died in a fire. He was crying and saying that they had to identify her from dental records and he never got to see the body

146

and I said that was what they did after fires and he started crying again and nodding and saying he knew. I held both his hands between my own and said, 'It's alright darling' over and over again.

A pause. Heartbeat black. I woke up on the rug in front of the fire, which was off. The light from the window was murky and all the lights were on. My head felt like a hot window-pane; not sore, but glaring. I stumbled frantically upstairs feeling odd, inexplicable pains in my legs and found Charlie asleep on the spare bed. I rolled him under the icy covers and crawled in beside him.

At first I'd want to know what happened and Charlie would screw up his eyes as if it pained him. Soon enough I learnt that I didn't really want to know. My memories of weekends became like scrambled knitting, full of gaping holes caused by dropped stitches.

I'd lie in the bath and wonder where bruises came from. I must have fallen over or been pulled to my feet. I burnt off a chunk of hair once, I think using someone's lighter, and I cut both my knees to shreds falling out someone's car.

My mother got to hear things, which greatly embarrassed me. She'd come round and scowl at Charlie and give me one of her evasive little talkings-to. I had to pull myself together or God knows where I'd end up. I couldn't wait for her to leave, especially if I had a hangover.

And I told myself it was alright and things were in hand. I hadn't missed a class, well, only as many as anyone else and I was still making good progress. And there were still weekends when I actually gave the whole thing a miss. I'd go to Julia's and we'd get in some wine but that would be all and I'd just stay over because I knew Charlie would be out somewhere and not due back till the morning.

We became very close, she and I. Alcohol, in moderation, served as a kind of crowbar into confession and confidences. And

147

yet, the more we opened up to each other, the more we seemed to polarise. The more I talked about leaving, the more confirmed she became about staying. We seemed to shore up each other's self-image, defining it by opposition.

'But you can't,' I'd say, when she said she'd end up marrying Bob.

'But I will,' she vowed, though without a trace of joy.

We used to do that thing that me and Corrie used to do. Lie on our backs, side by side, and visualise who we'd be in ten years' time.

'Right. I've got long hair, down to my shoulders, and it's in really good condition,' she'd begin.

'OK, well, I've got even longer hair, down to my waist, and it's dyed black like Morticia's.'

'You bloody Goth! OK, I'm really thin and I'm wearing size eight jeans and I live in a Georgian manor house with roaring fires and collies. And it's just been featured in *Country Life*.'

'I live in a bijou garden flat in Notting Hill Gate and my next door neighbour is Glenda Jackson and she's just lent me a cup of sugar and said that my boyfriend, who is Pete Murphy from Bauhaus, is a bit of alright but obviously sooo in love with me it makes her sick.'

And so it would go on, till we'd run out of wine, sickened ourselves of coffee, finished the cigarettes and reluctantly resigned ourselves to bed.

On Saturdays, if I'd stayed over, we'd have 'Jerry Hall days', when we'd eat her mother out of fruit and do the whole face-pack, hair conditioning, leg-shaving thing. I'd return home at tea-time, blotchy and pale, and Charlie would look at me askance, saying, 'You look . . . er . . . clean.'

There was payback for all this, of course. Never mind the hangovers, the bumps, bruises and burns, the memory blanks and lack of money. There were the depressions. They were the worst.

Some dark mornings I'd wake up and wish I hadn't. The problem with alcohol is it collapses time and you can wake up on a Sunday morning and feel that it's only been the blink of an eye since the last Sunday. Everything in between a dark chaos with moments of lucidity punctuating it like a strobe-light across a street riot.

We were so bleak some days alone together that I wondered if I should just run and catch the next bus and go wherever it took me. I never said this to Charlie because I think it would have destroyed him. He felt it was his fault that things got so out of hand and I suppose it was in a way but I didn't want to be with anyone else, or even on my own, so it was my fault too.

'I wouldn't blame you if you wanted to leave,' he said on more than one occasion. And I'd look at him through the grey fug of headache and nausea and wonder where he thought I'd find the energy.

As you'd expect, our sex-life was hardly improved by this state of affairs.

Weeks could go by and the nearest we'd get to touching would be leaning on each other in bars.

But not always. Some nights, afternoons even, we'd suddenly look at each other or I'd sit down beside him and feel his hand brushing my cheek. No matter how hungover or grey he looked, I was never appalled, nor he by me. When we made love, I remembered what we were all about and it made him instantly happy and full of optimism. It didn't always have that effect on me though. Once or twice I'd hear the insistent whine of the wind under the doors or look at our brightly painted walls turned maudlin in the creeping winter light and wonder where on earth we thought we were going.

This must have been on my mind the night the Terrible Unmentionable Thing happened. Not that I did it on purpose, or maybe I did. I can't remember the whys and wherefores of it.

We began at a party at Long Lizzie's. We'd been at hers countless times but the difference this time was that there were some young people there. I mean, about my age, not tiny tots. And I settled beside them for a while, leaving Charlie with some old mate of his, gassing about someone who was seriously ill. I'd no idea who.

149

It was really fun actually. I'd not been in such light-hearted company for ages and certainly never when this drunk and full of false confidence. There was a guy called Ally, that I'd been to school with, and his sister Maureen, who'd already been married and divorced, despite being only twenty-one. She wore Gloria Vanderbilt jeans and a white blouse and I thought her the epitome of all I wanted to be. So skinny and smartly dressed and the way she dismissed men fascinated me. I was hooked.

Ally suggested we move on to his mate Gordon's house and I looked round for Charlie and couldn't find him.

Lizzie, who was sitting enthroned on a beaten-up Parker Knoll recliner, patted my thigh and said, 'You go on, pet. I'll let him know when he turns up.'

And so we were gone, marching up to an unfamiliar house, me with strangers and reeling with the novelty of it. I felt like one of a gang and I don't suppose I'd ever felt like that before.

I told Ally and Maureen about my classes and they seemed really impressed.

He worked on the oil rigs and made a packet, so he told me. 'But it's a shit life. It really is a shit life.'

Other people came and went and I was keeping a weather eye open for Charlie but, deep down, I didn't want him to turn up just yet. I was enjoying being with Ally. He had a terrible crew-cut but he was quite good-looking and very, very attentive.

'You're really something,' he said, and Maureen guffawed and sidled away.

Ally frowned, half-seriously, and said, 'I mean it. You're beautiful.'

I snorted and straightened my face. 'Go on,' I said.

'You're beautiful and smart. What are you doing stuck here? You could come to Aberdeen with me, I've got money.'

'You mean, be your kept woman?' I laughed.

Luckily we were interrupted at that point by Charlie, who looked at me quizzically and asked if I wanted a drink. Less luckily perhaps, we moved on to another party and I met up with Ally again when I went to find the toilet.

'Ah, the vanishing lady,' he said, and the guys he had been talking to melted into the wallpaper.

We ended up in his car, just talking at first and then he suggested we go for a drive. To Gordon's now deserted house. Which is where it happened. Or rather, where I let it happen.

I don't remember the sex, just the awareness that it was going to happen and then it having happened. Waking up to a bedside lamp with an unfamiliar head between me and the light.

'Charlie?' I asked, stupidly.

'No, Ally,' he replied sleepily. And then he sat up and looked at me, asking if I was OK and rubbing his eyes.

'Did we?'

He nodded. 'Was that guy your boyfriend?' I nodded and covered my face with my hands.

'Can I see you again?' he said miserably.

I shook my head and realised I was going to cry. 'Shit', he said, stroking my hair in awkward little gestures, 'I'm sorry.'

'Not your fault,' I murmured, and began to pick up my clothes. It took me ages to get out of that house, I was so bleary and disorientated. Ally kept offering to drive me home and I shook my head vehemently, labouring under the notion that that really would be the last straw as far as Charlie was concerned. God, whenever I thought about him I wanted to whimper, I was so alarmed by what I had done.

I didn't even say goodbye to Ally. I just hoped he was due offshore immediately.

Charlie was sound asleep in bed when I got in. At least, he seemed to be asleep. If he wasn't, he sure as hell wasn't waking up for me. I looked at his face beside me as I lay there, not daring to take my clothes off, and willed him to open his eyes even though I was terrified of how he would look at me when he did.

When he did, he was sitting up, fully dressed, looking down at me. I closed my eyes for a second in shame and when I looked again he was leaving the room.

'Charlie . . .'

He stopped. 'What?' He sounded angry.

'I'm sorry?'

151

'Well I'm not. I'm not even surprised. Maybe he's your better option.' His voice was tailing off in a confused crackle and I sat up and saw, to my horror, that he was weeping. I don't mean crying, I mean weeping like the world had come to an end.

'Fuck you,' he wailed and was gone. I didn't see him for three days.

He arrived back during the night of the Tuesday. I heard him stumble through the door and, at first, I thought there was someone with him but he was actually just swearing to himself. It was hardly the most propitious moment to have that talk, so I tried to go back to sleep but actually lay awake half the night listening out for him.

I must have slept because he was beside me in the morning. Which I was grateful for. He couldn't hate me that much; it couldn't be over if he was willing to share a bed with me. Then again, shouldn't I have been more considerate and slept in the spare room?

I crept out of bed and took clothes with me onto the landing where I got dressed, trying to make as little noise as possible. The weather sounded ominous – shards of hail threw themselves against the windows – but I still went out and walked.

I wandered to the holiday park, which was almost deserted. A few seasonal workers were renting, you could see by the gas cylinders at the doors, but they were either sound asleep or off to work by then. I walked up to our sad little chalet and looked in the window. Nothing. It looked like no one had ever lived there, there was no trace of us left.

Then I went all the way down to the sea and watched what had now become rain pinprick the waves as they lolled across the shingle. I saw a light go on in someone's house on the mainland and I wished I was that person, getting up to a normal day in an established life.

And then I saw the most peculiar thing. I thought it was a buoy at first, black and bobbing in the water. Then I thought it was a man wearing a black swimming cap, ploughing steadily through the icy water, not raising his face. Then I saw it was a creature, an animal of some sort.

As it got nearer and nearer my part of the shore I became more and more baffled by what it was. A round, long head, a bit like a hippo's, and oily black shoulders, labouring forwards. Suddenly it broke surface, its bulky body battling with the weight of the water. I saw its legs. They were short and ended in trotters that skidded and struggled over the stones. It was a giant black pig, with horns at its snout. I looked at it in incredulity and it looked back at me with the same expression.

'Go! Get going, go!' I whispered and it turned and ran, stumbling up the bank, across the road, and into the trees beyond.

In the dreamy half-light of that morning it occurred to me that, if a wild boar could swim a stretch of sea, you couldn't rule anything out.

I went home after that, my jaw still slack with amazement quite possibly. Charlie got up from the kitchen table and walked towards me. I flinched involuntarily and he said, sounding wounded, 'I'm not going to hit you. I would never do that.'

'I know,' I said.

And he took me in his arms and buried his face in my hair, saying, 'I thought you'd gone.'

27

It wasn't quite the instant reconciliation it seemed. We stood like that for maybe three minutes and then didn't touch each other again for about a month.

Charlie was lovely but even he couldn't remain unmoved by such an insulting and hurtful slap in the face.

I asked him if he hated me maybe some thousand times and he would shake his head and ask if I was sure it wasn't me who hated him.

I felt permanently sick and my guts bubbled and sputtered like a Victorian water heater, emitting somewhat inappropriate gurgling noises throughout our sombre tea-drinking sessions. Of course, we drank alcohol too. We drank whisky till our feet and hands went numb and then went silently to bed where we lay, our bodies touching but in an almost hostile way. His body heat actually making me feel colder.

It rapidly became unbearable and I took to charging out of the house at random moments in order to march to random places in a bid to feel, if not better, at least different.

Charlie barely left the house. Once I even thought about setting fire to it simply to get him to move. But I realised he was so deathly depressed, he might just stay put and let the flames have their way with him.

I missed three weeks of school and got a letter from the headmaster, enquiring – rather spitefully, I thought – if I intended to return. I phoned him from the café and said I had flu but would have stopped having flu, probably, by Monday. He responded to this call as if it was the most gracious and well-mannered encounter of his lifetime. Maybe I wasn't imagining it after all – maybe all his other pupils really were unlikeable psychopaths.

With a grisly heart I returned to *Hamlet*, that most soulless of ponderers, while Charlie sat behind me like a brooding sunset.

I couldn't have read more than four lines before I turned on him and shouted, 'Are you ever going to talk to me again? Or are you just waiting for me to go?'

He shrugged and carried on reading the paper – God, he could lose himself in those freesheets! – and then crumpled it all up and glared at me and shrugged again.

'Well?' I shouted, getting to my feet because having to turn my neck three-hundred-and-sixty degrees to see him detracted from the forcefulness of my bearing.

He shouted back. 'Well what? What do you want? Are you honestly telling me that this . . . here . . .' – he gestured at the lilac walls, rendered glumly lavender in the drab afternoon light, and the battered sofa strewn with newspaper and streaks of cigarette ash – 'is what you're really after?'

I nodded my head vigorously, swaying slightly in the aftermath of the action so that I had to feel for the table to steady myself. Charlie observed this closely, his brow furrowed.

When he spoke again, his voice was clotted with genuine misery.

'Maybe you'd be happier with someone else. Someone younger, like that . . . that guy.' Here he flicked his hand at me in a violent little gesture that made me jump. 'I'm not a great catch, I can't give you the kind of life you want.'

I tried to interrupt but he shook his head at me and I stared at him in surprise.

'I know what you're going to say. You're going to say that this is better than living with your mother, or living like Julia, or Suzanna, or Lorraine and it is. By miles. But they're not you. It doesn't matter about them. But it does matter about you.'

155

He paused. I would have got a word in – had I been able to think of one – but he started up again.

'I don't think this is what you want. I don't think it's enough. And . . . I don't know, I don't know . . .'

A bubble of panic burst in my chest. Could this be it? Was he really going to go for it? But underneath the panic there was a tiny little shard of excitement. The door to the future was hanging wide open – all I had to do was walk through it. This could be it. If I didn't stop him, he'd finish us off.

But I couldn't let it happen. It would be like letting him strangle a dog we both loved just because its breath had gone bad.

I felt terribly sad and started swaying again while he looked at me intently.

'Don't,' was all I managed. The word sounded like an un-cooked bread roll.

'Don't?'

'Don't,' I repeated and went over to him and wrapped my arms round his shoulders. I felt his hand on my hair and I just willed him to shut the fuck up and let it be and, mercifully, he did.

Somehow we managed to be sorted without actually talking about anything.

For my part, I was glad to squirm my way out of gruesome Ally confessions. For selfish reasons, those of comfort mostly, I let it go unexpurgated. I think he let it lie for different reasons.

We stood in the middle of that shadowy room, holding onto each other without saying a word, until the shudder of the evening bus passing the front window broke the spell and we stood apart like teenage lovers after a first stab at coitus.

We bumbled through the next few days quite well, all things considered.

Charlie was horribly pale but his hilarity came back in fits and starts and we both stopped acting like we'd just heard the three-minute warning.

* * *

My dad wrote. He wanted to borrow back that £400 he'd sent me. I put his letter in the bin without even ripping it in half. It seemed more contemptuous that way.

So there we were, side by side, trying our damnedest to be optimistic. Every time we left the house together, something I tried to engineer we didn't do, my heart was in my mouth lest we run into Ally. Please God, let him be gone. I had this idea that Charlie would actually drop dead if we did meet him. And if he didn't, I'm sure I would.

We really cut down the drinking, but not for health reasons. We were afraid of what might transpire if we got seriously drunk together. That meant that Charlie went out on his own more, which I didn't greatly like but it seemed a safer option and it did wonders for my complexion missing all that booze. And my studies – I read so many books that winter, I'm sure I was eligible for some kind of book club award.

It was getting close on for Christmas and my mother was campaigning for us, or preferably just me, to spend it with her at Mary's. I couldn't think of anything I'd rather not do – apart from have Ally join us, perhaps – and adopted a cross-eyed, stupid look whenever she mentioned it. This invariably caused her to tut and change the subject, which was a result in anyone's books.

Even with Mary doing her impersonation of a roly-poly Dickensian cook with no end of pigeon pies and mincemeat fancies, it would still have had that post-apocalyptic tang to it, and anyway, I felt me and Charlie were too emotionally delicate for that kind of thing just then.

Which we were. He looked like he was tempted to impale himself on his fork when I mentioned it over some lukewarm, straight-from-the-packet fish pie.

He remarked, as he scraped half his dinner into the bin, 'You never did learn to cook, did you?'

It took me an hour or two to work out what bothered me about that sentence.

157

'Past tense, Charlie. Don't talk about us in the past tense,' I said, sitting on his knee.

'Did I?' he said vaguely, lighting a cigarette without offering me one.

We even missed the thorn tree.

'It's all crap anyway,' said Charlie. 'The guy's wife ran a hotel.'

Oh.

28

M y dad wrote again, this time saying that he would be 'passing through'. I said to Charlie that I might as well give him the money back and he rounded on me, saying, 'Don't you fucking dare.'

Dad never did show up which made me suspect he had never intended doing anything so requiring of effort as to drive four-hundred-and-fifty miles north of London, even for the equivalent in pound notes.

'Lazy bastard,' I said aloud, and Charlie caught my eye and we smiled at each other.

Julia passed her driving test on the 21 December and Bob bought her a car the day after. It was the kind of gesture Bob would make – big, showy, emotionless. But she seemed happy enough with her big metal fume-machine and insisted I clamber aboard and accompany her to the mainland to do Christmas shopping, have a meal and get drunk. I had to point out that the latter part of this plan was unfeasible now that she was a driver and she laughed and said, 'Oh yeah. We'll have to do that when we get back then.'

She had a very practical streak and frequently reduced life to a To Do list in this way. Years later I began to wonder if it was ironic on her part, a way of taking control of her life by ridiculing it. I've often meant to ask but when we meet I feel stupid going over what was. We got through it, that was the main thing.

Suzanna loves all that, I'm told. She spreads her youth out on the carpet like a photo album and endlessly celebrates it, poor cow.

It was a wretched day, bright grey with a sky full of sleet and it was so cold that if you allowed your arms to unfold even a smidgeon the freezing air ran up and down your skin like shivering little spiders. I was wrapped up in so many layers I looked like a well-lagged boiler, and I'd even taken the precaution of filling a thermos full of tea. And packing some Wagon Wheels and cigarettes.

'Will you be OK, love?' said Charlie sarcastically as I set off.

'But it's so cold,' I bleated, and he gave me a big hug and said he knew what would warm me up and gave me a dirty wink. It had been ages since he'd said anything like that.

The journey to the ferry should have taken less than half an hour but it took over four times that. We stopped for petrol, for a cigarette – Julia hadn't achieved sufficient confidence to smoke and steer, for a cup of tea, countless times so that I could get out and spray de-icer all over the screen which would freeze over again within minutes and once, rather shockingly, for Julia to throw her hands over her eyes and burst into tears.

'What the hell's the matter?' I said, sounding censorious when I'd meant to be kind.

She shook her head behind the hands and her hair, springing loose from its armature of kirby grips, fell forward like the closing curtains on a stage. Her head kept shaking until, with a loud sniff, she rubbed away her tears with such vigour it looked sore, and started up the car again.

'I'm fine, honestly,' she said, and we drove on in silence.

The ferryman, a young man called Brian whose short brown hair looked like the stubble farmers burn at the end of the year, told us it was taking a risk to cross today. Julia fixed him with a stare and said we'd be fine and we finished off the tea and the biscuits waiting for him to agree to take us.

Which he did, slowly across a greaseproof paper sea that melded seamlessly with a greaseproof paper sky.

We sat in the car and smoked for dear life, making it look, to an outsider, like its upholstery was on fire.

When we arrived at the other end, Julia drove purposefully towards the main street, which was so tightly packed with cars and people it made me want to dive out the car window and swim for dear life. She swerved into a side-street emblazoned with double yellow lines and parked.

'You can't!' I screeched, 'Julia, you'll get a whacking great parking ticket.'

'Like it matters,' she said, slamming the door and marching off. She only agreed to come back and lock it when I told her the car would *definitely* be stolen if she didn't.

Then she led us off at Scout's Pace to the Town and Country Hotel, an establishment so drearily old-fashioned we were bound to get lunch, even at this time of the year. We even got a heater thanks to the slightly over-earnest attentions of the fifteen-year-old waiter who couldn't keep his eyes off Julia. I tried to regard her with a disinterested eye, looking at her red, wind-whipped cheeks and wild, springy hair, her dreadful quilted coat and her bouncy, spongy boots, and had to admit that, yes, under all that padding there was a perky little babe just scream-ing to get out.

I battled for a few minutes with my own inner resentment – no teenagers ever went bonkers over me, not even when I had make-up and a low-cut top on – before my natural graciousness returned. By which time, two wipe-clean menus had been slapped down on the sugar-gritted table top and Julia was talking about wine.

We negotiated it to the point that she could have one small glass of white if she ate her lunch and had a cake in the afternoon before setting off. She agreed and drank the thing in two swift draughts.

'Come on then, spit it out. What's the matter with you today?'

'Oh, nothing really,' she said, her eyes conveying quite the opposite.

I drummed my fingers and stared at her and she confided, very quietly, to the ashtray, 'I'm pregnant.'

At that moment our Tuna Melts – Julia's accompanied by sub-stantially more chips than mine – glided onto the table like two multi-coloured barges. I looked at them with hopeless bewilderment.

'Oh,' was all I could manage.

And, with a harsh brightness that made me think of nails scraping down blackboards, 'Is it Bob's?'

'Of course it is. Who else's would it be? God, I wish it was someone else's. If my mum knew or whatever, I know what she'd say but that's her look-out, you know what I mean?'

I had no idea. I nodded. And watched Julia tear into her food like a tigress at the throat of a gazelle.

She continued, 'I don't want it. I don't want to be pregnant so badly, I just can't believe it.'

'Will you, you know, get a termina . . . an abortion . . you know, get rid of it?'

She shrugged, and then rattled off like a Kalashnikov, 'Like that nurse, you mean? That would be two to his name. Two dead babies. It would make him so proud, so fucking cock of the fucking walk. Oh . . . I fucking hate him. Who told me I liked him? What fucking bastard told me I liked him?'

Him? Her mother? The both of them together? I kept my mouth shut, thank God.

She began to cry, snot running from her nose, while still shovelling a sizeable chunk of tuna and toasted cheese into her mouth. I found the sight rather touching and patted her forearm ineffectually without realising what I was doing.

Blowing her nose noisily on the festive serviette, she said, 'I've got money from my granny. She told me only to use it for something important and I think this is about as important as it gets.'

I nodded. I looked round at the specimens of humanity around us, old women with bad ankles making lethargic conversation with other old women. All those Bettys and Jeannies and Marys and Margos, the thick brown hosiery and tartan shopper brigade, they'd have been here too, crying their eyes out because the forces of procreation had made them pay through the nose – well, the womb actually – for being passive and not looking where they were going. Young women gone to grey.

Not this time though.

'So, you're really going to . . .?'

She looked at me directly, 'Oh yes.'

As we struggled through an odious gift shop called Posies – a place we always ended up in at this late stage of the season – I asked her if she was going to buy Bob a present.

'Like this, you mean?' she said, holding up a mug cast in the shape of two huge, ponderous, very yellow boobs, with nipples the colour and texture of maraschino cherries.

I laughed and she shook her head. 'I never buy him anything. He tells me not to. Mind you, so does my mum – but she means the opposite. Oh, I don't know, what are you doing?'

I showed her my sorry array. A teapot in the shape of an Aga, positively swathed in saucepans and cats, for my mum; a selection of miniature marmalades for Mary, and a toy cat wearing a red scarf for Charlie.

'Does Charlie like things like that?' she asked me as we packed our horrors into the boot of the car.

'No,' I laughed. Actually, I'd already bought him a collection of Seamus Heaney poems, a bottle of Laphraoig and three pairs of socks but this wasn't the time to start waxing lyrical about my love for Charlie.

Though of course I did love him. Of course I did.

Our return to the island was very comical apparently. Charlie told me he watched the car approach the village like a speeding ambulance, park abruptly at an angle, half on, half off the verge, and saw the two of us skedaddle into the pub like two paramedics at the scene of an accident. And fail to re-emerge till midnight.

'I did come down to join you but your eyes, both of you, were like crosses. I left you to it,' he said, trying to place a cup of tea in my shaking hands the following morning.

'Where's Julia?'

'Bob took her home, but I take it something's up with them?'

'How d'you mean?'

'Well, even more than usual, she looked like she wanted to sink ice-axes into his skull.'

I'd never noticed that before but he was right. Julia's body language, especially after a few drinks, had always been saying what she'd finally spat out in the Town and Country. But no one listened round there, not even me.

29

That January, Charlie and I went to hospital three times.

The first time was with Julia, who'd booked herself in for a termination at a private clinic in Glasgow. She started out by saying she would go alone but eventually I got her to agree to my coming and then to Charlie driving the car.

Bob didn't know what was going on. He saw we were suddenly, all three of us, as thick as thieves and he looked on angrily.

'He can go fuck himself,' said Charlie and all three of us laughed rather unhappily.

Julia moved all her things back to her mum's, who didn't know what was going on either, but she started sleeping in our spare room which, for her benefit, now had a feeble little electric heater installed in it.

'That'll keep the very ends of your fingernails warm,' I said, by way of apology.

Julia looked at it without seeming to see it and smiled. 'It's just fine.'

The private treatment cost her a lot of money but she said, 'Better than walling myself up alive.'

She got up late every morning and went to bed earlier and earlier. Her makeshift bed started to resemble the kind of nest a feral creature might make in an abandoned house, all tangled sheets and debris, socks and so on.

At one stage I swear her conscious day had shrunk to less than ten hours. And, ironically enough, she looked more and more tired the more she slept.

She complained that she had a horrible taste in her mouth all the time and her hair seemed to darken about seven shades.

Bob came round the second evening she was with us and asked to see her in a voice which suggested he'd rather stub cigarettes out on his knees.

I told him she was in the bath and he said, 'Never mind,' and hurried away.

I felt very sorry for Julia about that. A bit of resistance would have been nice. I watched him barrelling up the road towards his car, his big round head buried into his big round shoulders and thought, what a fat oaf. It was the best I could do, there was so little else to say about him.

The day of Julia's abortion we got up at five o'clock in the morning. When I was a little girl, lights on in dark winter houses always signalled frightening, adult emergencies. Illness, sudden death, desertion. Now here we were, in the middle of one of our own making. Though it still felt like playing at grown-ups – to me, anyway.

Charlie drove steadily through the darkness while Julia and me dozed in our seats.

Sometimes he stopped and talked to us like he was our dad. 'Who wants tea?' he'd ask, patting Julia's knee and, minutes later, he'd return to the car with three polystyrene cups guttering boiling orange brew.

An hour and a half later I woke up to find the darkness fallen away and the car caught up in a stream of early morning traffic filing along the motorway into Charing Cross.

I looked out at new-build offices and rusty tenements emerging from the blue backdrop of morning, as yellow squares of light flicked on in random succession. I looked along the string of red tail-lights disappearing into the tunnel and wondered what it must be like to be surrounded by all this movement and noise and light, all day, every day.

To be cheek by jowl with ten thousand people and sleep with

165

the hum of traffic and the orange haze of streetlights. It wasn't the city itself, it was all those people in it. People who didn't know me, people who would let me be new again. Somewhere in that Glasgow morning were the friends I would have in the future and the rooms I would sleep in.

I looked in at the faces inside cars as they pulled up beside us, wondering.

But then I looked at Charlie, the huge presence who'd filled up my life but who was also just a tiny little barnacle gripping a tiny little rock in the grand scheme of things, and told myself to shut up.

The implications of what I wanted didn't bear thinking about.

Julia leaned forward – she'd been crashed out across the back seat – and asked Charlie if, afterwards, he could drive past Queen Margaret College.

'Sure,' he said. He had his eyes on the traffic so he didn't see how feverishly animated she suddenly looked. Seconds later, she was asleep again.

The day passed unbearably slowly, for everyone I think. Charlie and me were too zombified with tiredness to do much and we couldn't fall back on that old favourite – steady, heavy drinking – because of the drive back. So we wandered through the city centre, getting hopelessly lost about a dozen times and finally ending up in a pub where we ordered lunch and tried not to fall asleep while eating it.

It was a dark, cavernous place with a clientèle consisting mainly of people who had been out shopping in cut-price stores and had decided, before they went home, to get absolutely hammered. It was very oppressive and the burgers and chips tasted like wood-pulp. I never went there again, not all the years I lived in that city. I think it would have broken my heart to remember Charlie's face, so worn out and yet so scared, like Richard Gere was about to step out the shadows and whisk me away from him.

He wanted me to hate the place, to see it as a squalid dead-end, but it wasn't in him to be that deceitful.

Later he bundled me into a taxi and we found ourselves standing at the front of the Gilmorehill building looking down

166

at Kelvingrove Art Gallery while a violet dusk quickened around us. He told me he'd come here when he was my age. The wind was blowing his hair this way and that and he looked very boyish and shabby, as if no one had ever taken care of him.

He told me he'd been going to study engineering but because he hadn't finished school he never got the Highers he needed. I'd look after him, I told myself. It would all be alright.

'I'm sorry,' was all I said out loud.

He raised his eyebrows but kept looking outwards at the park and the shivering trees. 'So am I,' he said.

There was a beat of profound silence and then he started hee-hawing with laughter.

'What . . . ?' I wondered, in that bemused, uncertain way you do when you think someone's been taking the mickey for the last ten minutes.

He could barely contain himself and kept wiping tears from his eyes.

'When I was twelve, right, I was going to write this book,' he gasped at last, 'And it was going to be called . . . *The Last Summer*, and it was about . . . oh God, it was about this horse . . .'

Now I was laughing, with no idea of why. A horse?

'This horse that had been given a . . . ahaha . . . year to live and the novel was going to be about its last summer.'

He paused to take a deep breath and continued more soberly, 'The thing is . . . I've no idea what I thought I was going to fill the pages with . . . I don't know, what he had for breakfast? Whether he managed a little gallop in the afternoon? I mean, no idea . . . All I knew was that he would die very slowly – and sadly – at the end.'

Still laughing, he put his arm round my shoulders and gave me a hug.

'Jesus Christ, I haven't thought about that in years. I don't know where that came from.'

We collected Julia at seven o'clock. She was surprisingly alert and, if not smiling, not wretched either.

167

'I'd still like to see Queen Margaret College,' she said, even though it was dark.

Charlie nodded and followed the little map she showed him, printed on the back of a leaflet. He stopped the car across the street from an uninspiring, brown exterior with the words spelled out in grubby white letters.

We sat in silence for a minute or two, until Julia said, 'That's great thanks. Let's go home.'

She slept all the way and we tucked her in that night under so many blankets and duvets that she said she woke up thinking there must be dogs sleeping on the bed with her.

She moved back in with her mother the next night. I didn't blame her. At least she had the benefit of central heating. And she finished with Bob the same night. Over the phone like a heartless bitch, according to her mum. I began to think she might actually be going places.

The second time we visited hospital was after me and Charlie had a fight, brought on by drink. We were fine on the surface but our real emotions were thrashing around under the surface like sharks under glass.

He told me I should fuck off or something, I can't remember, and I threw an empty bottle at him. It shattered on his head and his face was instantly covered in blood.

The next morning we drove into casualty and he got three stitches under his eye.

The scar, when it eventually healed into one, actually suited him. The violence didn't.

'Don't let's become one of those couples,' I pleaded. But we already were.

The third time we visited hospital was at the very dog-end of the month. Neil had been admitted with liver failure and everyone was calling to see him because, there was no doubt about it, he was going to die.

30

'So what did you think of Glasgow then?' my mum asked for about the nine hundredth time, so preoccupied was she watching Mary handstitch a hem on a new green and gold curtain.

'So neat. My mother never taught me anything,' she said and Mary looked up and smiled.

'It was dark and cold,' I said, trying to vary my answers in the interests of, well, interest.

'I've always liked it, much more than I liked Dundee. It was your Dad who wanted us to live there, not me.'

I asked her why she didn't think about going there herself. I didn't mean it in a cheeky way, but she took it like that and our mother-and-daughter bliss shattered like a dropped light bulb once again.

But I did wonder what she had in mind, long-term plan-wise. I was supposed to be the drifter, I was the right age and had all the right qualifications, not my mum. When I said anything to Mary, she'd simply smile at me and say Ira would be alright, I didn't need to worry about her.

I wasn't worried. I was just curious.

Neil died. When we went to see him he was the colour and texture of yellowed paper. Like a book left open by a window all summer. I could hear his breath whistle through him when he tried to talk and noticed that his black beard had turned the rusty grey colour of old nails.

Charlie was deeply upset about it, I hadn't expected him to be quite so grief-stricken. I hadn't expected him to be grief-stricken at all; I thought he'd just be a bit glum.

Even odder, his brother came down the road and took Charlie out for a drink. I watched them go with my jaw on the floor. I wondered, for a crazy moment, if Neil was their dad or something, I just didn't get it.

I tried to be supportive and help Charlie but he seemed intent on making me feel that this was nothing to do with me. Right enough, I couldn't exactly stand there singing the deceased's praises because the only thing I knew about him was that he drank more than anyone I'd ever seen in my whole life. And he had that weird beard.

The funeral was to be the following Monday and I looked forward to it because I hoped it would dispel the pall cast over us by this strange little man's demise.

It seemed to have fallen to Charlie and Alistair to organise the service and, honestly, it wouldn't have surprised me if Alistair had dug out the grave with his bare hands while Charlie donned a top hat and sang the psalms accompanied by a cinema organ, the whole thing was so inexplicable.

'Why are you two responsible for it all?' I kept asking, as I watched them being brothers for once. 'Charlie?'

'I'll tell you all about it, I promise,' he said, as someone else knocked on the door to offer their condolences.

'I've heard that one before,' I said, without bothering to disguise the note of peevishness in my voice.

There were three days of this. I was seventy-five pages behind with *For Whom the Bell Tolls* but I couldn't settle to it with the floodtide of sorrowful souls that washed up on our doorstep all hours of the day and night.

But on Sunday morning, when Alistair had gone home, Charlie surprised me by asking if I would help him clear out Neil's house.

'Will I need this?' I enquired, flourishing a packet of Flash, and he nodded grimly, 'As much as you've got.'

The house stank, there's no other word for it. I'd been there

170

before, quite recently in fact, but it had descended into unbelievable squalor. As soon as Charlie opened the door I could smell a kind of caged animal smell that made you want to breathe through your mouth except you were afraid of what might fly into it.

Charlie opened all the windows and I walked slowly into the kitchen where I could hear bluebottles ganging up around the light, which was still on. Half a loaf of white bread had fallen into the sink where the tap dripped water onto it.

As I reached it I knocked over an empty bottle which set off a chain reaction, like dominoes, of clattering glass.

'I'll clear up in here,' said Charlie from the door, 'There's bound to be maggots.'

So I went into the bathroom, where I began blindly stuffing ancient deodorants and shaving foam aerosols into a Presto carrier bag and flushed the toilet a dozen times to get the water to run clear.

I felt as if my skin was crawling with insects. Every time I picked something up I had this impression of scuttling and it set me off in a frenzy of cleaning.

I scrubbed at the cracked sink, scouring at membranes of filth and as I leaned down to wash the inside of the bath I tried not to imagine the many-legged things that might be dropping onto the back of my head from the ceiling.

The water turned from brown to lemon yellow as the last spiders' legs washed down the plug-hole and I turned to the floor.

As I struggled with an ancient mop that seemed to spread dirt rather than absorb any I realised Charlie was beside me.

I was sweating heavily with the effort I'd been making and my fingers had wrinkled up into white prunes with all the undiluted detergent.

'Thanks for this,' he said. 'If you really hate being here, I can finish up myself.'

'Oh no, I'm just getting started.'

We did get it done. We went round that sorry little house filling bin-bags with everything we could get our hands on. There was

171

nothing of value – Neil's life was a collection of newspapers and old bottles, a tragic brown suit and ashtrays nicked from pubs.

On a mantelpiece in a backroom I found a picture of a solemn woman in her thirties maybe, wearing a buttoned up coat and holding the hands of two boys. One, the younger, looked up at the camera baring his teeth in a little boy grin while the other's face was slightly blurred, like he looked up at the wrong moment.

'That's me,' said Charlie when I showed it to him, 'The blurred one.'

'And that's . . .'

'Mum, and Ali.'

We kept the photograph but everything else we piled up in the back garden, for a bonfire another day.

'He used to take us in, when Dad got too much. He, Dad that is, would get pretty violent when he'd had too much and the first we'd know about it was Mum bundling us along to Neil's in the middle of the night.'

The light was nearly gone but we sat on in Neil's living-room, drinking the wine I'd run along to the Drumclair for. The sofa was the colour of gravy and I noticed worn patches in the carpet through which you could see the ghosts of floorboards.

'I used to love it when we came here. I was just wee. I didn't realise what was going on, it seemed like an adventure every time. We had our own room, in the back there, where he kept the bed made up, and all three of us would sleep bundled up like badgers – as Neil used to say.'

'What was he like then?' I asked wondering, bizarrely, if the beard came later.

Charlie grinned, 'Like a big badger. A big hairy badger.'

Neil, I discovered, had wanted Charlie's mum and the boys to come and live with him. 'He'd have done anything for her.' On numerous occasions he took them to the ferry, buying them tickets for Glasgow, Liverpool, even London, 'and all we ever did was reach the mainland, have fish and chips, and come home again. Sometimes he was still there when we got back, bouncing

172

up and down with frustration. But he would take us home again, and then rescue us again, and then take us home again.

'It must have driven him out of his mind.'

Charlie poured out the last of the wine just as the gas fire puttered out.

'That's the end of Neil's housekeeping then,' he said, adding rapidly, 'He didn't drink until after Mum died. I think he kind of felt like he'd played his hand and lost and that was that.'

'He just gave up?'

'Sometimes people do.'

That night I woke up to find Charlie lying on his back. My hand was on his chest and he was holding it between both of his. Something about his pose made me guess that he had recently kissed it. He must have kissed me when I was asleep, not looking for a response.

To love me was, for Charlie, a straightforward, no questions asked matter. Like children who love running and just break into a run for no reason other than that they like it. Just like that, Charlie loved me. He liked it, he did it, that was all. I didn't even need to love him back.

'You're the best thing I've ever had in my life,' he once said.

I looked at him that night and realised it was true.

31

N eil was buried the next day.
    A nasty squall came on during the early hours of the morning and by the time they carried him to the graveside the wind was howling like damned souls. Then again, it could just have been damned souls. It was the perfect weather for it.

Of the funeral party, only Charlie wore black. Everyone else turned up in a mismatched array of sombre browns and blues, the men in ugly shirts that gaped at the neck or had to be worn with the top button undone, their feet encased in unfeasibly shiny shoes that still smelled of their box.

The minister's words were whipped into the sky as soon as they left his mouth and his handful of earth blew across the coffin top and across the front row of leatherette toes. The clouds above us heaved with unspilt rain and the gravediggers were anxious to get started before the earth turned into a quagmire.

I didn't notice at first that there was someone new among us. Everyone looked unfamiliar in their Sunday faces but I noticed her when she approached Charlie and took both his hands in hers.

'I'm sorry,' said Kate, as I felt Louise put an arm around me and steer me towards her car. We drove in silence to their house which, set high above the village, seemed to be the only place not swathed in black cloud. David once told me the house was two-hundred-and-thirty metres above sea level and ever since, I'd imagined the air to be thinner and clearer up there.

And you could look down and see the whole coastline, rimmed

in gritty shore and lacy white surf. It made you feel like you were standing on a rock in the middle of the sea. Which, I suppose, was exactly what you were doing.

David was standing at the door with his daughter in his arms. She was fast asleep, her tiny mouth chewing away at nothing. He smiled at me, and back at her, then asked if I was OK.

'Yeah,' I said, burrowing my finger into the tiny pink hand and feeling the fingers gently clasp it. Her eyes momentarily squeezed open and a little bubble of saliva popped at the corner of her mouth.

And I asked if he was OK – and Lorraine.

'Och, you know,' he said, meaning not really.

'She should be inside,' said Louise, in a voice that wasn't even paying attention to what it was saying.

'She's fine,' said David, in a calm, fatherly way that surprised me. We were all, I saw, growing up.

I waited at the door with him, anxious for Charlie.

'Kate's here,' I said and he said, 'I know.'

And, 'She's staying with us. But don't worry about it, there's nothing left between her and Charlie any more.'

'There better not be,' I grinned.

'There isn't,' he grinned back, 'Anyway, he'd have to be bonkers.'

They arrived in the same car and Charlie leapt out as soon as it stopped.

'This is Kate,' he said, and I shook hands with the tall, well-built woman in the navy-blue suit whose wicked blue eyes showed up how much the rest of her beauty had faded. Her body looked heavy with disappointment and her feet, squeezed into court shoes, looked lumpy and sore.

She led the way into the house, her head down.

Charlie and I followed, him glancing at me from under his hair like a West Highland terrier that's just eaten the butter.

'Is there any reason why I should want to punch your lights out?' I asked casually.

'No-o-oh,' he said, in tones of mild outrage.

'Well then, stop looking at me like there is.'

*   *   *

Contrary to expectation, Kate's presence didn't disturb me at all. I'd imagined that, when our paths crossed, I'd become jittery and bitchy and end up passing out over my own sick. As it was, I was sleepily bored as early as the first circuit of the rickety gold hostess trolley that bore ludicrously large whiskies and what looked like quarts of sherry.

Poor old Charlie was getting his ear bent by a succession of elderly people whose faces lit up with dusty animation when he did them the honour of replying. Some of them, I suspect, only got this level of social interaction about once every three Christmasses, and only then if they'd had a heart attack. And they were determined to make the most of this lovely young man with all his own teeth and hair.

Charlie looked very young beside them. It amazed me that I'd ever thought him old.

Even when he was holding Marianne he looked young. The glow from her face seemed to reflect in his and I suddenly wondered why he and Kate had never had children, or why, assuming there were reasons, he'd never wanted us to.

Well, he'd not even wanted us to get married so I suppose that was my answer.

He was determined to be a dead-end, the last of his family line, and he obviously didn't feel any obligation to explain it to me. God, it annoyed me all of a sudden. To me! I was supposed to be sharing his life, wasn't I? And, what's more, I wasn't even twenty years old yet. What if his stubborn plans didn't suit me?

What indeed.

I took the baby from him for another clumsy attempt at child-holding and our eyes met. The expression in his suggested he knew what I'd been thinking.

'I just often wonder,' I said sharply, and he nodded, looking rather sorry, 'I know.'

Julia never made it to the wake. She'd been in church for the service and then hurried out without a word at the end. It wasn't like her, so I thought she was maybe still a bit under the weather.

Bob appeared though. With a girl no one knew and everyone ignored. Funerals, even more than weddings I think, bring out the clannish bigots in even the mildest of people.

'Where's Julia? I like Julia,' I heard more than several old ladies very rudely say upon meeting the dim, unsuspecting creature who'd actually said yes when Bob suggested accompanying him to the funeral of an alcoholic by way of a first date.

She chewed the tips of her sallow hair in her confusion as Bob quickly got drunk and fell asleep on a sofa. Social alienation was not something he dealt with adeptly.

The time passed very slowly at first, to the chime of tea-cups and glasses and an old man asking repeatedly if I was Jennifer. Then it speeded up as the drink took hold.

Louise told me I wouldn't know what had hit me when I had a baby of my own – like I currently had someone else's? – and every gin and tonic seemed always to be a half-inch away from empty, even though a succession of men kept refilling it.

Charlie hovered close by but I felt like I was trying to snare a fly when I tried to make him stop and talk to me. One question from me (generally of the uncontroversial, 'how are you?' variety), followed by one answer from him ('fine'), and he'd be gone. Disappearing into the crowd like a social butterfly at an Oscar Wilde theme party. I would have slapped him if he'd stood still long enough.

The worst of it was that, while he seemed intent on avoiding me, his former wife seemed intent on the opposite. We performed a sort of free-form madrigal for over an hour. I would nearly step towards her, she would respond, and I'd hastily step back. In the end, I gave up on Charlie and latched onto Jocky and David.

'Is your mum a lezzy?' asked Jocky, not unkindly.

I stared at him. I had no idea what he was talking about.

'I've no idea,' I said.

'It's alright Karen. Nor has he,' said David and Jocky shrugged, again not unkindly, and handed me a can of lager. It tasted wonderfully refreshing after all those bone-dry gin and tonics. My mouth felt like a parched sea-cave suddenly flooded by a freak-tide and I resolved to stick to beer for the rest of my life. I was sufficiently diverted by this mildly interesting musing that I didn't notice Jocky clearing his throat nervously.

'Julia's away,' he suddenly sang out.

'Eh?' I said.

'She's away. I drove her, I mean, she asked me to drive her to the ferry and see her off. She would have waited to speak to you but, with Charlie and the funeral and all that, she thought it better . . . she left you a note.'

He handed me a bruised blue envelope, the letters spattered with blobs of rain, and I sat down virtually where I stood, at the bottom of the stairs, to read.

David and Jocky looked on and then resumed talking in a respectful, visiting-a-church manner.

Julia wrote:

Dear Karen,

Letters are not my strong point so I won't go on. I'm off to live in Glasgow with a cousin of mine called Anne. I've never met her before and she sounds like a right bag – my mum likes her, enough said – but at least it's not here and at least she can't throw me out on the streets if I can't pay the rent. Don't worry, my mum's paying that!

I'm going to go to college next year and be a nurse. It may not sound like much of an ambition to someone like you who can pass Highers but it's a huge thing for me. It's becoming President of America for me.

I'm going to be a woman who earns her own money – and then marry a rich, handsome surgeon of course!

Bob and me we're finished as you know!! I feel fine and just wish I hadn't wasted my time with him.

I also want to say thanks to you and to Charlie. I don't know what I'd have done, particularly without you and even though I live somewhere else now I'm always here for you and I hope we're always going to be friends. You were always the best one and the one who listened and I won't forget that.

Don't think too badly of me.

Your wayfaring friend,

Julia

She had added, in a wobbly, I'm-in-a-car script:

PS: I would have stopped to say goodbye but there was a guy in a black suit who looked like he needed you more.

*   *   *

It was a sweet note. I was pleased for her. No, I was absolutely fucking chuffed out my brain for her. Go girl, I thought. I looked up and both the boys were looking quizzically down at me. I smiled and they smiled.

'Good,' said Jocky, and we all had another beer.

That was the nice bit.

The day went darker from there on in.

David went to attend to Marianne, Jocky was cuffed round the ear by some badgering matron and sent to pour drinks and I made a false move somewhere near the sideboard and ended up face-to-face in a furniture cul-de-sac with Kate.

God knows what she'd been drinking – petrol perhaps. Whatever it was, she had suddenly become deliriously drunk and her face was mottled and red, like she'd just had it in a fire.

She lit a cigarette, taking her leisure now that I was trapped, and eyed me through her haze of smoke.

'I take it no one's told you about him,' she said, her chin up and her eyes narrowed. She seemed to regard herself as some kind of latter day Marlene Dietrich and me as a schoolgirl in need of a good talking to. I was very tempted to stick my tongue out.

'Whatever,' I shrugged and made to walk away as rudely as I could, but she grabbed my arm and pronounced, 'You should listen to me. No one will tell you what I wish to fuck they'd told me.'

The expletive jarred so much with the rest of her that I was stung into paying attention. Who says the odd swear word can't be effective?

She continued in a softer – but not very sad, despite what she said – voice, 'I know it's very sad about his parents. It was really awful and I can't imagine what it must have been like for him. But the fact is, what happened when he was little wasn't my fault – and it isn't yours.'

'I know. But he doesn't take it out on me. He doesn't even talk about it,' I said, sounding high pitched and petulant.

She suddenly lurched backwards and I caught her by the arm. For all that she looked like she'd slept in her clothes, I could feel rich wool under my fingers and noticed her wristwatch was a Cartier. In some place other than this she clearly was somebody.

And even though she was completely pissed, half of me wanted to hear her out. I don't know why. Horrid fascination, maybe. I don't know.

She muttered about being sorry and resumed an upright position while lighting another cigarette. I discreetly doused the one she had left burning on the top of a beer can.

Shaking her head as if to wake herself up she continued, 'He's a lovely man, he really is. When I left I missed him so much, I'd have done anything to go back . . . but I couldn't.'

Her eyes brimmed with tears that were quickly recalled, like a glass of gin threatening to tip over and righting itself just in time.

'I had the choice of being with him. Drunk all the time. Not having kids and not having money or hope. Or leaving – and I left.'

'Hmm,' I said, by way of discouragement. It was like listening to my mother.

She vigorously snatched up the slack in our conversation. 'I look a mess to you, I can see that,' nodding at my midriff which was rather trim at the time, 'but I have a house and a job where people respect me and I get paid good money. Bloody good money, and it probably sounds very dull and suburban – you're young, you probably have other ideas – but it's much more than I'd ever have had with Charlie.'

She was right, it did sound dull. But so, I knew, did mine.

Louise appeared and attempted to steady Kate by jerking her elbow so violently she nearly went flying.

'Steady on,' she said, 'How many have you had?'

Kate looked confusedly at her empty glass. 'Three?' she ventured. And at me, 'I hardly touch a drop these days. Thank God, you must be saying, if that's what it does to her. I got all my drinking done with Charlie.' And she cackled fondly, causing me a painful jab of jealousy. I didn't want her to be fond of Charlie. That was my job.

I think the bitch noticed my discomfort because she said, in a nasty little voice, 'I was a New Start too, you know. A whole new

180

beginning. And I was the first, so I was the one he tried the hardest with.'

She paused to take in breath before launching into her next volley, 'But that's his problem – he never gets beyond these new beginnings of his. He's mired in his dreary, drunken old man past and he'll take you right back there with him.'

I snatched her glass from her, said, 'I think you've had enough' and marched away indignantly. It was my way of trying to make her feel as bad as I did.

Stupid bitch, I thought. Was her suburban, swollen-ankled life so fucking disappointing that she had to come back here and make herself feel better by insisting she was the love of Charlie McGuigan's life? Fuck right off.

But that wasn't her game and I knew it.

I found myself clinging to the back of an empty chair like I'd just been washed up by the sea and this was the only rock in sight.

It didn't get any better.

Charlie was sitting hunched in an armchair, wearing his crosses-for-eyes look.

Generally I found this endearing but that night it was infuriating. Especially as I suspected it was a put-on to stop me trying for meaningful conversation. I tried to work out what this kind of carry-on reminded me of and realised it was David – as a teenager.

'What's the matter with you?' I hissed, unwittingly attracting the attention of several dozen bleary eyes.

Charlie shrugged, grinned, said 'Nothing' and came within a hair's breadth of being whacked across the face by me.

I marched off to the kitchen where I helped myself to an entire plateful of mini sausage rolls and waited for him to follow. He didn't. The last time I looked, he was still stuck to that chair with some bladdered old bird, with a cleavage like two wrinkled crab apples, perched precariously on the arm. To his credit, he didn't appear to be enjoying the attention. After that, I took my leave.

If he woke up on the floor alone, then that was his problem.

32

The blue night sky was as clear as polished glass. Moonlight glanced off frosty tarmac and bare branches and it was utterly, eerily silent. The only sounds were those of my feet crunching along the road and the very distant, possibly imagined, barking of a dog.

I felt alone and quite giddy with it, like a toddler who's slipped away from his mum for five minutes – just before he gets scared and starts bubbling at the security guard. For the first and only time I wondered if I should leave Charlie. If, after all, I'd be happier without him. I was probably weaving all over that road, hiccupping drunkenly, but I remember my state of mind as being very cool and clear. Like polished glass.

In the house I made myself a cup of coffee, which I took upstairs to bed. I drank it and promptly fell asleep. Before I did so I promised myself solemnly that this really was it, that that alcohol-free week I'd planned so long ago was now beginning. My liver could begin the clean-out job now.

He woke me up less than an hour later. At first I thought he'd been hit by a car because he was soaking and my half-conscious brain took it to be blood.

Outside the rain was pelting down. The clouds must have come from nowhere to shatter my pristine night, and Charlie was wet from head to foot.

'Are you OK?' I asked, scrabbling upright and instinctively putting my arms round him.

He nodded and I saw, once I'd switched on the light and established that he wasn't fatally injured, that he was crying. Or had been. His face was raw.

'I love you so much,' he finally said, his words all smudged.

'Have you done something?' I wondered. He seemed so changed from the slightly smug person I'd abandoned at the wake. He shook his head and put his hand over his eyes as a choking kind of sob rose up from his chest.

'Was thinking about my mother,' he seemed to say. I couldn't quite hear him. I waited and he gradually came to, as it were.

Looking at me directly, he said, 'We won't ever get married or have children. It's not fair and I'm sorry.'

I waited.

'It's not you, it's not me being afraid of commitment or any of that . . . shit. It's . . . I can't do that to you.'

Sitting up, I tried to take his sodden jacket off but he resisted.

'Stop it, Charlie. You're scaring me.' And he was. I could feel my heart beginning to go and I wanted him to lie down beside me and tell me everything was OK. I didn't know what he was on about and I didn't care.

'Doesn't matter,' I kept saying, 'We're OK, we'll be OK,' and he kept shaking his head and looking at me.

Then he touched my cheek, so tenderly that the tears sprang from their ducts like sentries caught slumbering.

'I love you so much, and I always, always will,' he told me.

And then he stood up.

'Where are you going?' I whimpered.

He flung his arm out abstractedly.

'Just a walk. Clear my head. You go to sleep.'

He sounded casual, but I didn't like it. I watched him stumble heavily to the door and bump down the stairs. The front door shut with a decisive click.

I lay back feeling my heart beat like a bomb in my chest.

*   *   *

183

In the morning I woke up staring at my bare arm stretched out across an expanse of bare bed. Charlie hadn't returned.

I remember hurling myself out of bed and into a pair of jeans and a jumper like a manic cartoon character – all my movements seemed to happen at top speed and in mid-air. My pulse was racing so fast I thought it would choke me.

Oh God, oh God, oh God. What's happening, what's happening.

Downstairs I felt that the furniture was crouched in readiness for me. It knew – how long before I did? Will she work it out? The air felt static with event.

I stamped on the floor, as if to make it stop, and shouted out, at the top of my voice, like a howl, 'Charlie!' But I knew he couldn't hear me and I knew he'd never hear my voice again.

He left me a letter. It just said goodbye. It had four hundred quid tucked inside it.

I sat down at the kitchen table with the two ripped halves of the Miro poster in my hands. Fuck him. I thought, well, I'll wait, I'll fucking wait.

My mum came round and put her hand on the crown of my head and pulled it to her shoulder. And I cried and cried and cried and she went 'Shhhhhh' but actually meant, make as much noise as you can.

I had diarrhoea for ten days. It doesn't sound like the most Greek classical way to pine but I felt that my innards had gone into mourning and that, in their grief, they were spitting out every-thing that was good for them. My skin went very white and spots broke out all over my neck and shoulders.

'Look what you're doing to me, Charlie,' I said into the mirror and watched as my face pulled itself down like a mask of tragedy.

I was so angry and so hurt and so lonely and all I could think about was how much I loved him.

184

Epilogue

I t's been over twenty years since I last saw him. For a long,
long time I waited.

I stayed in his house all that spring and summer but no one saw
hide nor hair of him. I was still waiting even when I moved to
Glasgow. I looked into the faces of people in the street, to see if
one of them was Charlie. Even the phone, even the *phone* ringing
made me start, this man who'd never had a phone and had never
talked to me on a phone.

I did get away. I had to resit all my Highers at a college in Glasgow
because I failed across the board that summer. I spent a year working
in a fishmonger's shop that was so cold I didn't need to run up the
electricity bills when I got home because, by virtue of having the
door closed, it was ten times warmer than my place of employment.

I ate a lot of fish and I caught a lot of colds and I felt like I
limped or something because I felt my heart to be so irrevocably
broken.

You don't want to know the rest. I did well – eventually. I got
married, I had children, I did all those things. And a damn sight
better than Kate did them, quite frankly. I never forgave her.
Whenever I remember her I shout out, if not audibly, 'Stupid
bitch.' I think there's got to be one person you never forgive – it
means you can forgive the others.

*   *   *

Julia became a midwife and she's the size of a house. She says midwives should be built like brick shit-houses. It reassures the patient. She married an unbelievably handsome paramedic and they've had no kids because he's got some hereditary disease in the family.

Mum lives with Mary. Dad lives with himself – no one else could.

I still think about Charlie. I think about him a lot. My husband gets annoyed about it every now and then and jokes, rather angrily, that it's like competing with a dead man. 'Dead men can't make mistakes.' For all I know he is competing with a dead man.

I stopped looking, you see, when I became afraid of what I might find. Maybe in a ditch, maybe dead. He was listed as an officially missing person for years and now he's presumed dead, I suppose. I'm not sure what I think.

But he made me feel like a better person and so I became a better person. It was the very least I could do for him.